THE BLOW-OFF
LETTER AND
OTHER
FABULOUS TALES

DAVID LASTINGER

The Blow-Off Letter and Other Fabulous Tales

Copyright © 2021 by David Lastinger

ISBN: 978-1-7368578-1-6

This book is a work of fiction. Names, characters, business, events and incidents are the products of the author's imagination. Any resemblance to actual persons, living or dead, or actual events is purely coincidental.

Cover creation by Ravi Verma from rdezines

Developmental editing by Emma O' Connell

Editing and formatting by Lorraine Reguly from https://wordingwell.com

Dedication

I would like to dedicate this book to all of the people that helped me write it—Anne (my wife), my family, and my friends.

A special shout-out to all of the strangers whose paths crossed mine. You didn't know that your silly antics were going to make good story material.

Table of Contents

DAVID LASTINGER

Tale #1: A Midnight Stroll through the Woods

It was the middle of January, and the snow around Mark's Rocky Mountain cabin blanketed the area in majestic whiteness. Every morning after new snow had fallen, it was exciting to see the deer and bunny tracks all over his property.

Tonight, he was planning an unforgettable night. His girlfriend, Katie, was coming up from the city. Due to their busy schedules, they didn't see each other as much as they would have liked. They had been together since college, and finally, three years after graduation, they were able to work in the same town. Katie didn't know that he had a couple of surprises and some good news for her tonight.

He finished cleaning up, lit some candles, and had just opened a bottle of wine when the doorbell rang. The porch light illuminated the flakes of snow in Katie's hair. It had started snowing again. When she reminded him that it was cold and snowy outside, Mark realized he was simply staring at her. He gulped, grinned sheepishly, and let her in. She thought it was cute and started laughing.

He put on some music and they sat down for dinner. Mark had some pretty good skills in the kitchen department, as he'd spent several years working in various restaurants while he put himself through college.

Katie loved coming over to eat because she wasn't that good of a cook and was always too busy to make a reasonable effort at it. Tonight's menu included Caesar salad and pasta. The smell of freshly baked sourdough bread wafted through the house.

Mark was a ski instructor at the local ski mountain. Katie was a Doctor of Physical Therapy (DPT). They talked and laughed about the day's events. It was not a big town, and quite often, they had the same clients. She would hear all about how mean Instructor Mark had made them crash. He was always yelling something about a pie wedge. What the heck did food have to do with skiing, anyway? *(Note: A pie wedge is the move that you make to stop when you are on snow. It's usually the first lesson taught. Some might not deploy it well and fall down or crash. They are usually harmless falls, as they occur on a wide-open bunny slope.)*

The big news Mark told Katie over dinner was that he had been promoted to Director of Skiing that morning. He would now oversee all the rentals, retail, and instruction. It was a big deal, with a nice jump in pay, to boot. She was excited for him and knew he was a perfect match for the job.

When dinner was over, Katie started cleaning up in the kitchen. Mark started the coffee then went outside to get some more firewood. A short while later, a fire was lit and roaring in the fireplace, the dishes were done, and Mark and Katie enjoyed some coffee and Kahlúa on the divan behind the bearskin rug that lay on the floor in front of the burning logs.

Before they knew it, they had talked and laughed their way to midnight, and they were feeling the effects of the booze. The full moon brightened a window and caught Katie's eye. When she looked outside, she noticed that the snow had stopped falling.

Mark winked mischievously, stood up, and said, "Get your coat. Let's go for a walk. There is something you need to see."

They bundled up and headed out the back door. The moon was high in the sky and cast a heavenly glow over the trees. Mark took her hand and led her toward an old, cross-country skiing trail that disappeared into the forest.

All was quiet except for the snow crunching under their boots.

"Where are we going?" Katie asked.

"It's a surprise."

Another surprise? What is this guy up to? Katie wondered. She was a curious lady and hated not knowing a secret.

Mark just smiled at her, and the twinkle in his eye told her that she would have to wait. They walked in silence for another few minutes until they reached the surprise, which made Katie gasp and squeeze his hand.

What she saw was a very unusual tree standing in a clearing by itself. As local legend went, Mark explained, a mysterious person would walk through the woods every year and choose a solitary tree to decorate. It was never the same one twice.

Many of the townspeople thought it was old Henry Stevens, one of the original town founders. He was a bachelor who had never had a family to celebrate Christmas with. Whoever it was, the mystery person usually picked a tree that seemed lonely and bare, as if it wanted to look as beautiful as the other trees in the forest.

The brush had been cleared from underneath this one and was replaced with a plaid tree skirt. Ribbons and bows of all sizes and colors were tied to the branches. The decorative balls that hung from the branches were also unique. Each one was made from either popcorn or birdseed so that the visiting deer, rabbits, and squirrels could enjoy them as a snack. The final piece that tied it all together was the angel that was fashioned from the branches found on the forest floor and secured to the top of the tree with more colorful ribbons.

To complete the scene, a handmade bench was nearby for visitors to sit on and admire the tree and listen to the woods. The bench was made by one of the local Boy Scouts.

Katie and Mark sat on the bench for a while in silence, hand in hand, just taking in the whole picture and enjoying the serenity of the moment. Katie had never seen anything like this, and she turned around to give Mark a great hug. She whispered in his ear that this was one of the reasons she had fallen in love with him and gave him a soft, warm kiss.

Mark reached into his pocket and pulled out a little blue box.

"Katie, you know that I'm not good with this kind of stuff, so just bear with me. I'm sure you know that I have been in love with you since the first day I met you. I'm pretty sure you feel the same way." He got down on one knee in the crunchy snow, opened the little box, and asked, "Will you marry me?"

Katie fell to her knees to join him on the ground. She hugged him and said, "Oh, yes! A thousand times, yes! I've been waiting for this day, too!"

Mark was tingling as they walked back to the cabin with their arms around each other and the ring on Katie's finger. He couldn't help but feel that Old Man Stevens was looking on from somewhere, smiling his approval.

DAVID LASTINGER

Tale #2: The Secret of the Airplane Pilots

Captain Andrew was a retired commercial airline pilot who had put in his years in the cockpit and had looked forward to retirement.

After a year of playing golf, hanging out with all of the other retirees, and even eating at home fairly regularly, he was bored. He missed the action of being out and about as well as the freedom of flying.

One of his pilot friends, Frank, had a small plane just sitting in his hangar. It was not getting flown as much as he had hoped. He was too busy with his daytime job and didn't have time to fly for fun. Once Frank heard Andrew's story, Frank told Andrew he could fly it anytime he wanted. He just had to pay for the gas.

Needless to say, this thrilled Captain Andrew and it wasn't long before he and Captain Frank met at the local municipal airport for an introductory flight. The short trip from Phoenix to Sedona was comedically known as "the hundred-dollar hamburger flight" due to it taking $100 in aviation fuel to make the trip. Everything went well and before Andrew knew it, he was making plans for future adventures.

One day, he got a call from the local Humane Society, who said they needed a rescued Golden Retriever to be transported from Phoenix to

Sacramento. They couldn't pay him for the trip but Andrew agreed to help because he was allowed to take the expenses off of his taxes as a charitable flight—the icing on the cake, as far as the Captain was concerned.

The rescue coordinator had found a couple in Sacramento who had seen the dog online. They and their child immediately fell in love with him. It happens that way with Goldens and their famous smiles. Arrangements were made. The couple even paid for everything upfront, even the flight.

On the morning of the flight, Andrew got the plane prepped and fueled up. He was getting his flight plan filed when he accidentally bumped his head on a cabinet door he left open.

"Damn, that hurt!" He noticed a little bump but went on with his plans without another thought about it.

A few hours later, the Humane Society's coordinator met Andrew at the airport with his four-legged passenger, a two-year-old Golden Retriever named Clancy, who had been given up because his owner could no longer take care of him. The man had recently been admitted to a nursing home facility. Big dogs were not allowed there.

In typical Golden Retriever fashion, the furry creature greeted Captain Andrew with a lot of tail wagging, a big smile, and even a raised his paw.

The Captain cordially shook his paw. Once he got settled in, the coordinator gave the dog a mild sedative to make the trip a little easier on him.

Captain Andrew was now ready to go, so he fired up the Piper PA-46 Malibu and taxied out onto the runway. Once he received tower clearance, he was up and away—on his first solo flight in a very long time. After he got to cruising altitude, he was thankful for the pressurized cabin and the air conditioning. His passengers, four-legged *or* two-legged, would also appreciate that.

"So, nice plane you got here. It's pretty smooth back here, too."

The Captain looked around because he thought he heard someone talking. He gave his head a shake.

"You aren't believing what you are hearing, are ya?" Clancy asked.

Andrew decided to play along, still skeptical, thinking he would have his hearing checked once he got back to Phoenix.

"Okay, I'll bite. What's your name?"

"My name is Clancy. I am not sure how it is that we can understand each other right now, but I'll bet we have a great chat."

Andrew wasn't the religious type. However, he was spiritual and believed that this opportunity was presented to him for a reason. For that, who was he to ignore it? Who hasn't wanted to hear what a dog or any other animal had to say?

"So, Clancy, tell me about your previous owner."

"I am going to miss him a lot. He's had me since I was a pup. He was so much fun to be around. We went everywhere together. When I was old enough, he even took me fishing on his boat. Sitting at the front of the boat, splashing through the waves, was fantastic! Once in a while, I would help him get a hold of a fish or two."

He went on to talk about what had happened. "I noticed a change in him, long before anyone else did. I didn't know what it was called, but it wasn't good. I only wish that I could have told his family sooner. It was really tough to watch him steadily get worse. It was later that I heard the humans talking. They said it was Alzheimer's."

They continued to chat for a little while longer until Clancy fell asleep again.

About an hour before touchdown, Clancy woke up again with a big yawn.

"Ya know, normally, I would be really sad, but I heard that I am going to a young family. My owner would be proud of them for taking me in."

Once they landed at the airport, the new family was there to greet the pilot and their new best friend. The family invited Andrew to have dinner with them and stay overnight at their home. After the long flight, the hungry captain gladly accepted. It had been a while since he had had a good, home-cooked meal. Their little boy was almost five years old, full of boundless energy, and curious about everything. Clancy, being only two, had plenty of energy to keep up with the young fella.

***

After arriving back in Phoenix, the captain called up his buddy and invited him to lunch the next day.

When the two met up, Andrew told Frank he really had to talk to him. From the puzzled and apprehensive look on Andrew's face, Frank could tell that he had discovered the secret.

"So, they talk to you, too, huh?" Frank whispered and grinned.

"Holy crap, Frank! You should have told me! It damned near caused me to have a spell up there. I thought it was because I got a bump on my head after whacking it on a cabinet door!"

"Well, I thought about it, but declined, just in case you couldn't talk to them. You would have thought I was nuts. From what I can tell, it only works on the plane and nowhere else. I tried."

So, Andrew told him of the flight and what they had talked about. Frank wasn't sure if it worked with cats, as he hasn't flown with any. Both were curious to see if they talked, too.

Over the next year, Captain Andrew became the pilot of choice for his local Humane Society. Consequently, he has had many conversations with the animals he has transported—including dogs, cats, birds, and even a python.

Neither pilot has figured out why their powers only work in the air.

Tale #3: The Blow-Off Letter

This happened many years ago before the age of cellphones, pagers, and even online dating. Answering machines (if you had one) worked via a tiny cassette tape. I believe I was about 21 years old at the time.

I knew this girl, Mindy, in high school. She was much too pretty and exotic to be interested in me, let alone even know that I even existed. She was tall, of Spanish descent, and had long, flowing black hair, a beautiful smile, and the sexiest voice you can imagine. It was just the right amount of raspy, like you might hear from a blues singer. When I would see her walking in the hallways or in my classes, it always made me weak in the knees. Keep in mind, back then, I had no game.

High school graduation came and went. A few more years passed. Then, I ran into her while she was working at a local department store.

We stopped for a moment when we realized that we knew each other. I was extra surprised that Mindy remembered me.

Somehow, I mustered up the courage to ask her to lunch and was even more surprised when she said yes. We traded phone numbers. A few days later, we got together.

Being the nerd that I was, just being on a date was a great success. We traded stories and ended up having a great time.

After a few more dates, I finally kissed her. That was indeed a banner day—it was my first real kiss.

One of our dates was a trip to the Phoenix Zoo. It was a beautiful spring day in the middle of the week, so there weren't many people there. We were walking around, holding hands, and having a great time. Around the corner of one particular walkway, there was an ungodly noise, like none I had never heard before. Curious as to what it was, we both hurried around the corner to where the turtles display was. Lo and behold, there were two turtles having sex. The noise was coming from the fella on top. We turned a little red, started laughing, and went along our way, hoping to give them a little privacy.

A few months later, at the end of the summer, Mindy quit talking to me and would not return my phone calls. This came from out of the blue. I was perplexed; I didn't recall a fight or argument that might have led up to this.

Back then, all we had was a phone call (which was occasionally taken by an answering machine), a visit in person, or a letter in the mail. After a week or two of trying to contact her, I said, "To hell with this," and quit trying.

I didn't forget her right away, though; it would take a while to forget someone like her.

While I was thinking about how to put some closure on this wonderful chapter in my life, I had a brilliant idea, which was how the official blow-off letter came to be.

It started very formal and legal-sounding (written to the best of my ability) as I spelled out the reasons for and my feelings about it. It filled up a page. The letter went something like this:

Dear Mindy,

I sure would like to understand the reason you are no longer speaking to me. There is not a fight nor a cross word that I can recall we had. Your behavior is completely unexpected. You have ignored my messages and notes for the past three weeks. Sadly, you won't step up and tell me what is wrong.

With that in mind, this final letter is to let inform you that you have been officially blown off. I will no longer call, write, or try to contact you in any fashion.

I hope that you are okay and there is some sort of logical explanation for you acting this way. However, if you should come across a lake on your travels, please feel free to jump in.

Jerry

I attempted to hand-deliver the letter. Of course, no one was home, so I just stuck it in her mailbox. After that, I still tried hard to forget about her. Because we lived in nearby neighborhoods, it was possible but not probable that I might run into her again.

One day, the probable happened. When I realized she was standing in the checkout line in front of me at the grocery store, I could not believe my luck. Now, what to do about it? Not wanting to make a scene or anything else that might create drama, I had two choices available: I could just slink back into another part of the store and wait it out or I could quietly line up behind her. I was truly ready to check out myself.

She didn't see me behind her. The cashier was nearly through her full cart of groceries when Mindy happened to glance behind her and see me. Her eyes flew wide open as I quietly smiled and waved at her. Her next move surprised everyone in line.

She dropped her things immediately and bolted out of the store, leaving all of her groceries behind. The clerk looked at me for some sort of explanation. I just smiled, shrugged my shoulders, and said that she had recently dumped me.

The last thing I saw of her was her old Gremlin as it tried to squeal out of the parking lot. My last thought was that she had gotten and read the blow-off letter. *Mission accomplished!*

Many years later, after the introduction of Facebook, she sent me a friend request, out of the blue. Although I was shocked, I waited a couple of days before accepting it. Briefly, we caught up online. It turned out that she was living on the other side of town. Because I really wanted to know the rest of the story, and because my wife was also curious, I invited Mindy to have a drink with me—twice. She refused both times. About two weeks later, I unfriended her for good.

As I went to sleep that night, I wondered what a better outcome might have looked like, if I hadn't met my wife instead.

Because you never know what life will throw at you, as long as you keep an open mind and are willing to take a leap of faith, life could be a helluva adventure!

Ever since the invitation showed up in the mail, Jerry was both nervous and excited about the prospect of going to his 20-year high school reunion. While he did okay in school and had a decent time while there, he wasn't the brightest or most popular student in his class.

All of his high school friends had scattered to the winds after graduation, so keeping in touch with them proved to be difficult. It seemed they just didn't write back as often as he had hoped. Eventually, he gave up and went on with his life.

When it came to dating in high school, Jerry just didn't. He was growing at an awkward rate; he was tall and skinny, wore unfashionable plastic glasses, and sported a comb-over haircut. Plus, he was deathly afraid of talking to girls about anything other than schoolwork, which was tolerable but not comfortable. To make things more complicated, he had the same growing-up feelings as the popular guys. He was going through puberty, and all that came with it, such as a squeaky voice when he got excited.

One girl from high school always stood out from the crowd: Mindy. She, too, was not popular, but everyone liked her as she was friendly and smart.

Day after day, all senior year, Jerry sat two desks away from her. It might as well have been two miles because he was too terrified to talk to her. Of course, they said hi to each other, but that's about as far as his shyness and fear would take him.

Once he got into college, he decided that it was about time to up his social game. He was voted into an executive position with the Residence Hall Association. One of the perks of the RHA job was that he got paid. He also joined an intramural volleyball team because he loved the sport and figured it would be a good way to meet people who had a similar interest.

Social media had not existed when Jerry was in high school, or even for the first couple of years of college. Once it became more mainstream, he was able to catch up to his old friends and see what they had been up to. It was the same old story: some had done well, some had not, and some even passed away too soon.

One day, Jerry got an interesting piece of snail mail: an invitation to his high school reunion. He read it over a few times and finally decided that he would go. He had gotten older and wiser, and was not so afraid of girls anymore. He registered online and saw that Mindy was going as well.

The reunion was taking place at a fancy resort over the whole weekend with activities and events to attend prior to the big party on Saturday night.

He booked a room for himself and took stock of his wardrobe. He wasn't a fashion mogul but he was not going to show up looking shabby. The week of the event, he visited a fancy department store and enlisted the help of a personal shopper, who helped him put together some smart-looking outfits that would work for the event as well as the rest of the year. The shopper was a young lady. Surprising himself, he felt comfortable enough around her to tell her about the reunion and the girl he was hoping to run in to.

To his surprise, Jerry received a message from Mindy through the reunion web page. It said that she was looking forward to catching up with him.

Now, he was nervous and excited at the same time. How could she have remembered him all this time, and why? Didn't she like the other guys better? What did she look like now? *A million other thoughts went through his head.*

He arrived at the resort early Friday evening. After showering, he got dressed and went down to the opening reception. He thought he had changed a lot, yet his old friends recognized him at once. He was greeted warmly by all of them.

After getting a drink from the bar, he continued catching up with his old buddies. The tales and stories of their youth were now as big as the fish that got away.

All of a sudden, Jerry felt a tap on the shoulder. Turning around, he saw that it was Mindy. He was speechless; she looked even prettier now than she did in high school. For what seemed like forever, he just tried to think of what to say and pick his jaw up from the ground.

A few seconds later, she broke the ice with a warm hug, and said, with a twinkle in her eye, "I was hoping you would show up. You've been on my mind for a while now."

Pulling himself together, Jerry got drinks for both of them and they sat down in some comfy chairs located a little bit away from the crowd. Finally, being able to speak, they caught up on old times, shared what was currently going on in their lives, laughing and joking the whole time. He felt oddly more comfortable around her than he could ever recall, which was a big surprise to him, even after all these years.

The conversation stalled for just a moment when she looked him straight in the eyes and asked, "How come you never asked me out in high school?" Wow—not the question he was expecting!

However, he was now able to look her back in the eye and confidently tell her, "I always wanted to, but I couldn't even spell G-I-R-L back then. I knew that I wasn't cool enough to ask you, anyway. I wasn't popular, I didn't have a car, and I'm pretty sure you wouldn't go somewhere with me on the handlebars of my bike or have my dad drop us off at the mall!"

They laughed at that and then she surprised him even more.

"You should have asked. I would have been happy to go anywhere you wanted, handlebars or not."

Mind blown, again!

Right then, a few of her old girlfriends showed up. In typical girl fashion, they jumped up, hugged, and squealed in some foreign language that only girls know.

Before running off with them, Mindy said, "I'll be back later. Don't leave."

Jerry simply sat there, for a moment, processing what had just happened. The boys came over to get the story. He told them. In typical geek fashion, they were also amazed. Unanimously, they advised him to explore this more, to see where it goes.

The next morning, Jerry was still reeling from what happened last night.

What do I do about this? Where will this go? *He had been stung a few other times by the dreaded*

"R" word—rejection. It never feels good. For the geeks and nerds in the world, it hurts even more.

The reunion coordinator had arranged for a city ghost tour that afternoon, so he signed up. He had heard that they were lots of fun and you got to see parts of a city that you might not have known were there.

Much to his surprise, Mindy had signed up, too. She sat down in the seat next to him on the bus.

They had a great time on the tour. During some of the scarier moments, he found her holding his hand. It was electrifying to him and filled him with a feeling he hadn't felt before. Jerry wasn't sure where this was going, but he wasn't letting go either.

After the tour, with his newly-found confidence, he asked her if she would be his date for the big dance that night. She said yes. They then went off to their rooms to rest and start getting ready for the night.

Jerry was sure to wear the cool outfit the shopper had chosen for him: a pair of dark blue silk pants, a steely blue button-down shirt, a fun polka-dotted bow tie, and a beautiful pair of wingtip shoes. Before going to pick Mindy up, he stopped by the gift shop and bought some flowers for her.

Feeling very good about himself, he strolled down the hallway to her room.

He knocked on the door.

She answered it, wearing a long blue bathrobe and her silver-gray hair up in a ponytail. Mindy pulled him in, shut the door, wrapped her arms around him, and kissed him like he had never kissed before. Again, he was speechless and could not believe this was happening to him.

He felt warm and tingly as he kissed her back, holding her face softly in his hands. She let her robe fall to the floor as she loosened his tie and unbuttoned his shirt. He let his hands wander down her back, then around and up to her soft breasts. She caught her breath as he began to suck on her perky nipples. She reached down and finished undressing him as he continued to nibble on her breasts. As his pants hit the ground, she slowly stroked his rapidly rising cock.

After 20 years of wondering what this moment would be like, it was finally upon him.

He kicked off his shoes and they made their way over to the bed. As they fell onto it, he felt a softness and warmth that he had never known possible.

Many hours later, they discovered that they had missed the big party. Jerry had no regrets, whatsoever. They were having their own reunion!

The next morning, over breakfast, they discovered that they had more in common than previously thought. They both agreed that they wanted to keep seeing each other to see where things would go. It turned out that they really didn't live that far from each other and weekend trips were certainly possible.

As they left to go back to their homes, Jerry could not have had a bigger smile on his face. He was looking forward to a new adventure.

Six months later, Jerry and Mindy found themselves engaged to be married, much to the shock and delight of their friends and family.

When they wed, they held the ceremony at the same resort as their special reunion.

Tale #4: The Coffee Shop Adventure

It was about 10:00 a.m. when she came strolling into my coffee shop on Main Street. The morning rush was over, allowing me to usually have a little more time to chat with the customers. It was my favorite part of the day.

She was 5'8" and had long, dirty blonde hair. She sat a table near the window after the barista served her. By peeking at her coffee cup, I could see her name was Christy.

She was just in town for the day and had some time to kill before her appointment. Along with her coffee, she got a peanut butter cookie. I am famous around the county for these and they run out fast. There was a résumé on the table with her. I asked who she was interviewing with. It was Tom Thompson, the CEO of Gecko Enterprises, the biggest employer in town. She was applying for a position as his Administration Assistant.

"Oh, yeah, I know him. He's a regular. A really nice guy." He provided jobs for a lot of people in the county. They seemed to like working for him.

"If you get the job, I know lots of people who can help you with finding a place to stay, with moving, with whatever you need."

"Ah, well, thanks for that, and the cookie was great. I'm headed off to my appointment now. It was nice to meet you."

A few hours later, she walked back into my shop and said that she had gotten the job. However, it wasn't a full-time position, so she wondered if I had any openings for a part-time barista.

"Well, I might. Tell me a little about yourself. While you are doing that, make us two *doppio campanas*."

She went behind the bar, grabbed an apron, and in no time at all, had the coffees up on the countertop. I was impressed.

"Come on over here and let's chat." I retrieved the beverages and sat down at a table that offered some privacy.

She followed me over with two more cookies in her hand.

"You seem to know your way around a kitchen. What's got you looking for an admin desk job?

Between sips, Christy said, "It's a long story and I'd rather not get started on that one yet."

"I get it. No problem. Say, what are you doing early Saturday morning? If nothing, I have a big catering event. I'll need some help in the kitchen, preparing food. Think you might be interested in a little side job?"

"You bet! I will be here," she said.

On Saturday, Christy showed up at 5:00 a.m. and we got to work on the baking orders for the party. While we were working, she told me her story.

"I used to bake with my mom when I was in grade school and high school. It seemed like I was pretty good at it, so my teachers recommended I apply for the Culinary Management Program at Johnson and Wales College. From there, I worked as a baker in a five-star resort in San Francisco for about five years. That's where I met my partner, who was a chef.

"We decided to open our own bistro in Fort Collins. We were doing well, busy on the weekends, and had good reviews on the local social media pages. Then, two years ago, I started getting calls from our vendors wondering where their checks were. Chef was in charge of that part. After some digging, I found out that he was skimming money and not paying the vendors. Shortly after that, he cleaned out the account and disappeared. No one ever saw him after that.

"That completely broke me, both financially and emotionally. I had put my heart and soul into that place, just to have it stolen. In order to take care of the vendors, I had to sell everything in the café and had nothing left over after that.

"My parents were very supportive and let me move in with them while I recovered from this horrible thing. It was kind of weird to be living with them again. My dad loved it and gained 10 pounds because I was doing the cooking and it is better than Mom's. I couldn't stay there forever, so this is me, digging myself out of my funk and trying to live again. Maybe the office job will wake me up a little bit."

Later that morning, Tom Thompson walked in to get his regular Saturday apple crisp and a coffee. He pushed his way to the front of the line. He saw Christy behind the counter and was surprised to see her there.

"What are you doing here? Aren't you starting with me on Monday morning?" Tom asked, somewhat curtly.

Christy replied, "I have the skills, and he needed the help, so we got to work."

In the interview, she had worn an outfit that covered the many tattoos on her arms and her hair had been up in a ponytail. This morning, she was a little more casual with her short sleeves and hair down. The CEO hadn't seen this side of her and was a little shocked. "Did you get those in prison?" he snarked.

"WHAT did you say? Did I hear you correctly?" Her eyes flew open wide as she was processing what she had just heard. It was certainly not what she was expecting, especially from a future boss.

"I was just joking." He tried backpedaling out of that remark.

"That is not something that you say to someone just because they have tattoos. I have never been to prison and you are completely out of line, joking or not!" She was fuming.

His last line before he picked up his order and left was, "Geez, you didn't have to go all mental on me. I was just kidding."

Everyone in the café, including myself, was dumbfounded. We had never seen that side of the CEO and there was some uncomfortable silence while we looked at each other.

"This is about to be my boss? I've got a funny feeling about him now. I will be Googling him when I get home later. Okay, let's get back to baking and make this day better."

Shortly after that, George Ottermayor, one of my favorite old customers, came up and proposed to her.

"Young lady, if you can cook like this, I'd love to marry you. Let it be known that I think your tattoos are cool."

Christy came around from the counter to give him a hug. "Oh, George, you are so sweet. If this doesn't work out, I may just have to take you up on your offer." She smiled and gave him a wink.

Before she left for the day, I made sure to tell her that she could have a job with me anytime she wanted. I still wanted to expand the business and she had what it took to help make that happen.

I didn't see her again until Monday afternoon. She walked in and marched up to the counter where I was standing. She had a very matter-of-fact and determined look on her face.

"Ya know, I don't even know what I was thinking about applying for that job and sitting at a desk all day. I must have been nuts. That guy is a jerk. Can I still take you up on your offer? Sit-down jobs just aren't my style."

I could not have wished for a better day. With a big smile on my face, I said, "Yes, ma'am! Let's go talk about your future. I am tickled to have you on board!"

Tale #5: The Wanderer

After his wife passed away and the celebration of life was over, Mike started the process of selling the house and getting ready for the next stage in his life. It had always been a dream to travel and explore the US, and this was a great opportunity to do so. He intended on starting on one side of the country and working his way across, on his own schedule, with no particular place to be at any time.

After his wife's death, he had no more family or ties to this town and just didn't see a need to be here any longer. It was going to be just him and his dog, wherever the wind blew them.

He wasn't filthy rich, so he would have to travel on a limited budget. While he wasn't financially the wisest, he had also never planned to retire. With his crazy life, he predicted he would be dead long before the subject of retirement came along. By his calculations, he would be dead before 60, anyway. Everyone that he knew that was old was either crippled or gravely sick. He also didn't see spending time in a nursing home going well for him. Mike never wanted to be a burden to someone for his health care or well-being.

He had no legacy or kids to live for, so what was the reason to try to live to be 106? None that he could see. Throughout the years, he would see people on the news who had made it to 100. They didn't look like they were in great health. He never understood people who fought like hell against cancer. They would spend millions to beat it or just eke out a few more years, only to succumb to the disease and leave a huge financial debt on any remaining family. It was not fair, nor his vision of living.

Now, if he could just figure out how to tap into his social security fund early.

He was still not sure what he would tell his own remaining friends and family about his adventure. He wasn't particularly close with his family, but he would tell them, eventually. Maybe he would send them a postcard or visit, if he was nearby. It was the friends in his town he would be saying goodbye to, although not permanently, but it might be a while before he would see them again. With the advent of social media, he would never be that far from them. He even decided he would start one of those podcasts or a blog to document and share his adventures.

Heading out on an adventure without his best friend would be the hardest thing to do. His friend was working in another country. Mike missed him more than anybody. They had been best friends since he was ten, had saved each other's lives at least twice, and never had a cross word between them.

With a pretty long list of places he wanted to go, Mike decided he would start in the Pacific Northwest. He had a really good friend up there, whom he had known since high school. Sandy was a tall, blonde, free-spirited woman and did very well at doing her own thing. They always had a good connection and had remained friends all of these years. Currently, she owned a curio shop in a touristy town in Oregon. Maybe she would even join him in his adventure!

They had traveled together before when they took a trip to the California Redwoods. She was the first one to step up and agree to go. Like Mike, she had no kids to stop her from going. As far as the future went, he would be lucky to find someone who would want to go on an adventure like the one he was planning.

Other places on his list included many of the famous and iconic auto racetracks in the US, such as Lime Rock, Laguna-Seca, Willow Springs, and Road America. They all had great camping areas and he might even be able to volunteer as a corner worker. That would be a grand way to get closer to the action.

Road trips were always a great comfort to him. There were stories about the people that came before him to build these highways and byways. He often wondered if they ever drove their families around and said, "Hey, look at that bridge. I built that and it's still standing."

In order to help cover his daily expenses, Mike decided on joining up with the Forest Service Work-Share program, where you agree to work or manage a campground for a time, and they let you camp there for free plus provide you with a little bit of a stipend. It sounded to him like a great way to get around the country and meet a bunch of like-minded people at the same time.

Let the journey begin!

Tale #6: We Got an "F" in Bar Scene 101

Back in the day, when we had just turned twenty-one, Brian and I felt obligated to hit the bars and do what twenty-one-year-old guys are supposed to do: try to pick up girls. This was long before the Internet and swipe-style dating apps. I'm pretty sure that we knew we didn't have any game, but try, we certainly did.

We read all of the magazines like *Cosmo*, *Elle*, etc., to gain as much of an edge as possible. We were scared to death. Most times, we couldn't get past the "g" in girls when it came to talking to them.

We would normally hit the bar around 8 p.m. and scan it to see who might look approachable. Well, just to clarify, approachable to us. This would be someone who looked like the "girl next door," certainly not some supermodel type, which equaled "high maintenance" to us. We had no time for that. Plus, if they were afraid to get some dirt on their hands or break a nail, that would not work either.

Girls would sit down next to or near us and shoot a look our way, or maybe not. Trying to follow the "guy book," we would ask the bartender what they were drinking and send them one. Then, the crime occurred: they would say, "Thanks," pick up their drinks, and scoot—not our way. Damn it.

We continued this repeatedly, for a whole summer, yet never once got a positive response.

We would even have a loud, geeky conversation between us about fake scientific theories just to see if anyone would take notice. It was great fun! If you could have heard the crap we spewed, you would have laughed.

If only Match and the other apps had existed back then, our odds might have been a little better. After that summer was over, we never used that approach again. Our conclusion at the end of it was that girls were mean. We didn't have time for that, either.

There was one date I went on—despite the low number of them—that made me wish I could get that time back. It was so long ago that I don't even remember her name now.

It was Valentine's Day. I knew this girl from the Residence Hall Association I was part of. Neither of us had a date. So, we figured it might be fun to go out for dinner. She was a pretty brunette who had lots of energy, and most people liked her.

We chose one of the common hangouts and met there. Like so many poor starving students, having a car was a luxury neither of us had, so walking was our mode of transportation.

We had dinner, which went well.

When we had a few drinks, things started going downhill for me. The more buzzed she got, the more she started singing songs from The Monkees. I could not stand that show or the band, and the fact that she was singing so enthusiastically made it all the worse. I couldn't even imagine kissing her now! As soon as we were done, I paid the bill and we headed out.

Once outside, I gave her a quick hug and we went our separate ways. As soon as she was out of sight and hearing range, I let out a "Yeesh!" and made some funny faces. I could not wait to get home and put this one behind me. To this day, I don't celebrate Valentine's Day—and am very lucky that my wife doesn't buy into the commercial holiday either.

Now, I didn't always strike out in the dating scene. I met Martha while we were on campus for the summer. I wasn't taking any classes, but I got a job in the dorms working for the various summer camps, for which they fed and paid me. It was hard to say no to that arrangement.

Martha was working as a cashier at one of the campus dining rooms, and we happened to flirt a lot when I went through her line for breakfast. She was a bubbly redhead and had a nice laugh. I don't remember what our first date was, but I do remember a few good ones.

One night, in particular, we were walking home from the bar. We were quite drunk and stumbling around. It just so happened that next to the university, there was a graveyard. There had always been rumors that it was haunted and that sort of thing. We decided it would be fun to take a shortcut through it at midnight, just for the hell of it. About halfway through, we stopped to make out. We found a grassy patch and sat down, so we wouldn't fall over so much. One thing led to another. Before we knew it, we were naked in the moonlight and doing it right there! Afterwards, took a short snooze. When we woke up and realized where we were, we got dressed as quickly as possible, then ran out of there, laughing the whole way home.

Months later, we went home for Thanksgiving. Brian and I had planned to rent some four-wheelers and play in the desert during that weekend. Martha had never ridden one and wanted to go, so we found one that was an automatic, as she didn't know how to shift yet.

The night before we were to go, it rained like crazy in town. My mom was surprised that we were still going to go out riding. Mothers— hmmm. Luckily, my mom loved Brian. I'm not sure what kind of magic he possessed. It didn't matter where we were going; as long as I said I was with Brian, I had a green light to go anywhere from my mom.

"Bye, Mom. We're going to hell!"

"Okay, as long as Brian goes with you!"

We had already rented the quads; we'd picked them up in the trailer and that was that. A little rain was not going to spoil our fun.

After an hour of teaching Martha how to ride her machine, we felt good enough to take her a little further into the desert. Things were great, until I found an open field that was now a big mud pit.

I got there well ahead of them and hid behind a large creosote bush, waiting for Brian to come by on his quad. As soon as he did, I hit the gas, and with both back tires, I completely roosted him, starting what would be an epic roost war for about an hour. Martha tried to get in on it, but her underpowered quad couldn't do much in that department.

When it was over, we each weighed an extra 75 pounds. It took a little bit to shake off all the mud.

Along that desert trail, it was common to come across abandoned mine shafts, even though they weren't always marked on the maps. Of course, we couldn't help but check them out. The last one we visited went in about a hundred yards. We left Martha outside to keep watch. We were halfway in when my flashlight swept over something odd. It was a freshly killed rabbit.

I hissed to Brian, "Fresh kill!" It was a reminder that we humans aren't the only ones who seek shelter from the desert climate. We booked it outside, as quickly as we could.

On the way back to the trailhead, we followed a fence line pretty closely. The terrain was pretty rough, with lots of ruts and bumps to get through. Brian was riding up front, Martha was in the middle, and I was bringing up the rear, keeping an eye on Martha. She seemed to be getting it.

I turned my head away for just a moment. In my peripheral vision, I saw the fence shake. I looked ahead just in time to see Martha launch off the front of her bike; she had zigged when she should have zagged. She went helmet-first into the fence. (Always wear your helmet!)

I stopped next to her. She was pretty banged up. The helmet had taken a good knock and her leg was hurting. Thankfully, nothing was broken or bleeding. As a boyfriend, I was concerned about whether she was okay and not seriously hurt. As an onlooker who saw it happen, it was funny as hell. It was a good thing she didn't see me laugh inside my helmet.

When I finally took her home, Martha got out of her wet, dirty jeans to see why her leg still hurt. She had a bruise the size of a ham steak. It was about six different colors.

Despite her leg hurting and her mom being really mad at me, she said that she had a great time. Looking back, I'm not so sure she was exactly straight with me. A month later, just after the semester was over, she broke up with me.

The weird thing was, after we were over, several friends commented that they hadn't thought she was right for me. *WTF? Why didn't you mention that earlier?* To add to the weirdness, it had turned out that Martha knew Mindy (the blow-off gal) from a national collegiate club they were in together. When I'd told her of the breakup story, she'd laughed—and laughed and laughed— because she knew exactly who I was talking about. She also confirmed that Mindy really was crazy, and it wasn't just me.

Women!

DAVID LASTINGER

Tale #7: PCT and the City Slickers

On a section of the Pacific Crest Trail, near Julian, California, I had dropped off my best friend, Brian, to start that leg of the trail while I went ahead to set up camp for the weekend.

The Pacific Crest Trail is an enormous trail that stretches from the border between Mexico and California and to the Washington/Canada border. All in all, it is about 2600 miles. There's a Forest Service campground near Julian, and we've always had good luck with such sites. They're clean, well maintained, and have running water with good showers. A good shower is a plus when you've been in the woods for three days all by yourself, which was a standard operation for us, as Brian is a thru-hiker. Our plan is to complete the 2600 miles from Mexico to Canada.

Many have asked why I don't do the hike with him. It would be fun to do so. However, someone has to drive the truck and set up camp. On the plus side, I like driving, recon, and camp cooking. Brian can barely cook to save his life. I have hiked some of the trails backward to meet Brian in the middle, to hike back with him or resupply him with food and water.

Oddly enough, as remote as some of the trail areas are, there is usually fairly decent reception for our cellphones and walkie-talkies. Using the two-way radios is how we keep in touch, even though Brian might be ten to twenty miles away.

They also come in handy when he is just a few miles out. Our communications allow me to know when to get dinner started and have his shot of Fireball whiskey ready for him.

Brian is pretty easy to cook for, as he doesn't need many spices or seasoning on his food. His simple tastes must have come from his parents.

I remember when we were Boy Scouts, his dad was our Scoutmaster for a while. His dad's idea of a salad was a wedge of iceberg lettuce and some thousand island dressing, also known as McDonald's secret sauce. If you added some semblance of a tomato, you were getting fancy then. I must say, I have turned out to be a pretty good camp cook.

I was in the Forest Service campground near Julian, and it was a pretty nice one. The tent sites were level. They had running water and even a proper firepit. However, I did have the misfortune of being placed next to a family that had no business whatsoever being out there.

One look at this family and their new, out-of-the-box gear—some of it still had the price tag on—and I knew it was going to be a long weekend. Brian would be on the trails for a few days, so it was just me in the camp.

Once they got their camp all set up, Dad, the macho camper man, built a huge fire in their pit. Only a few months ago, this entire area was closed due to a massive wildfire. Areas just beyond the campgrounds still showed signs of the burned and scarred forest.

He built the fire in the middle of the afternoon. Shortly after that, the whole family left to go into Julian for some wine tour or something of the like. By itself, that is not a big deal. The big deal was that he left his fire blazing and unattended. Criminal!

I waited about thirty minutes to be sure they were truly gone and then went over and doused his fire with about five gallons of water. It was out cold when I left, as it should have been.

Later that night, after I had made dinner, I saw the family light another fire, making some of those messy s'mores that beginners always think are part of the camping ritual. They fed the screaming kids, put them to bed, and soon turned in as well. Again, Dad left his fire blazing. (I am hating that guy right now).

I gave it thirty minutes to make sure they were all asleep. Again, I took another five gallons of water and doused it. I also made sure to soak all of their other wood, as a gentle reminder.

It would have been great to know if they were wondering what was happening to their fires.

The pesky campers had been taken care of, and the rest of the campground was now quiet, so it was time to lie back, stare at the moon through my tent, drift off, and maybe have a nice dream…

Bob's wife, Michelle, told him said she had to go out of town on Sunday for a week-long job conference. Usually, her company lets the spouses travel along, but not this time.

"Where are you going?"

"Denver."

"Oh, wow, you love that city. You'll have a great time."

"What are you going to do in the house while I'm gone?"

"Oh, you know, just work, take care of the dogs, and stuff."

She rolled her eyes at him and let out an all-knowing, "Hmm, yeah, whatever!"

Ladies, do you ever ask yourself what your man does in the house when they have it to themselves? Maybe you wanna know. Perhaps you don't. This has always been a secret, and I'm sure gals have the same sort of secret. Just like passing gas, they'll never admit to it.

Sunday morning came around, and Michelle caught an Uber to the airport. Bob was still asleep—or was he? He adored his wife and only wanted the best for her, but he couldn't wait to start his weekend by himself. Oh, did he have plans.

The first thing he did was to go to the bathroom without closing the door. As long as they had been together, he and Michelle always closed the door when taking care of business. You know what happens in there—you just don't need to see it. Many years ago, his nephew had had a crush on a charming girl in his school. He was at a house party with her once, and she stunk up the bathroom. He told his dad after the party that he could never look at her the same way again.

Now, it was time for a bowl of cereal. Bob strolled into the kitchen with boxers and socks instead of his usual robe or full set of pajamas. Because he'd seen it in a movie once, he grabbed a stainless-steel mixing bowl, emptied a whole box of Lucky Charms into it, and then grabbed not only the milk but the half-and-half, too.

Feeling the need to be somewhat productive, Bob started to do some laundry. They had a fancy machine that could figure out all of the colors and whites by itself. For the life of him, he still couldn't understand why Michelle insisted on separating them manually. He threw everything in, added detergent and softener, and hit the button. An hour and some more cereal-slurping later, it was time to transfer the clothes to the dryer. So far, so good; there was nothing to this laundry crap—but don't tell her, or she'll make you do it.

They lived in a great big house, with enough bathrooms for a "his" and a "her" bathroom. Of course, she got the fancy en suite, and he got the one down the hall. She wouldn't even let him touch hers because he was a stinky smelly guy and would wreck it. Well, right now, he was thinking "spa day"—something that this tough guy would never admit to, let alone permit the words to ever cross his lips. All of his construction buddies would kill him over that faux pas, then take his guy card away.

Lavender soaps, frilly scrubbies, and even a foot scraper came into play as he sat on the bench with both showerheads blasting him.

Thirty minutes and some wrinkled toes later, he got out and dressed in his favorite holey sweats. Checking the dryer, he found that his laundry looked and smelled good. It took him a few minutes to hang what could be hung up. The rest got shoved into a drawer. Folding underwear? Humph.

He'd always been curious about the deal with silk underwear, so he tried on a pair of Michelle's boy shorts. Oh, wow! Now, he knew. They felt great as he strutted around the room like a Vogue model.

As evening came around, Michelle called from her conference to check in and see that he hadn't burned down the house yet.

"Oh, it's all good. Just me and the dog napping and trying to figure out what to make for dinner. Okay, I love you, too. Gotta go!" He crawled into the king-sized bed and took up the whole middle while also throwing all twelve fancy pillows on *the floor. Sheesh, more fluff than he could handle. He fell asleep with the dog on the bed and a* Three Stooges *movie on the TV.*

The next morning, as he was getting ready for work, he noticed that his ordinarily white T-shirt seemed to fit a bit more snugly. It was also a little bit pink. So, he changed his mind and went casual with jeans and a golf shirt.

He dropped the rest of the clothes off at the dry cleaner in hopes that they could fix them. Michelle would never know, as long as he got rid of the wire hangers and plastic bags.

The rest of the week went pretty well until Saturday came along. Oh, crap—she was coming home today! Bob launched into extreme cleaning mode—sweeping, mopping, vacuuming—and he got it all done with thirty minutes to spare. He even had time to light a smelly candle before she walked in, and he'd arranged to have her favorite baked ziti delivered from their local restaurant down the street.

Michelle opened the door, gave him a big kiss, and then did a quick lap of the house. It all seemed in order—until she woke up the next morning to find a pair of slightly wrinkled boy shorts under the bed!

Back in the campground, I broke camp the next morning. As I was heading out, I stopped by the ranger's office to let them in on what I had been doing. Such people end up starting wildfires because they don't have a clue. She had a good laugh at that!

The ranger had already noticed them and was keeping her eye on them. She also said she would have a chat with them that morning. I would have loved to have been a bug on the tree to hear that one.

Tale #8: My Favorite Christmas Tradition

For as many years back as I can remember, Christmas Eve and the following morning were always my favorite parts of the holiday season. My parents would always send us off to bed early—too early, in my opinion, but they argued that Santa would not come if we weren't in bed on time.

Every time my mom would peek in to see if we were sleeping yet, I would fake being asleep. All I had to do was wait until they went to bed and turned their lights out. For good measure, I would wait another twenty minutes or so, just to make sure they weren't faking it either. Once I heard them snoring, I knew I was good to go.

Then, like an Army Ranger, I would crawl down the hallway so they wouldn't hear my footsteps. Once I had achieved that part of the mission, I could close the living room door and turn on only the tree lights. That was usually enough light to check out what Santa (Dad) had brought.

After a careful inspection of the loot, I would then relax on the couch and watch the tree lights flicker. Of course, this was all made better by the caramel lollipops from See's Candies that were waiting in our stockings.

Our first year in Arizona, Santa wanted to make it a special one. As always, I planned my mission accordingly. However, things were different that year. It was like Christmas had exploded all over the living room. There were both unwrapped and wrapped presents everywhere.

It must have been about 2 a.m. when I crawled back to my room. Excited, I woke up my brothers to tell them what I had seen. We then went to the living room together.

We discovered Santa had made a big mistake: he had left batteries in all of the remote-control cars he'd gotten for us. It didn't take long to figure out that they didn't work well on carpet. We thus broke down some of the moving boxes we had left over from our big move, fashioning roads from the kitchen into the living room.

We must have forgotten to be quiet, as we were having a grand time and making more noise than we probably should have.

The next thing we knew, Dad was stomping down the hallway in just his tighty-whities. (Jeez, we didn't need to see that, and for the life of me, I can't unsee it! After that, I swore to wear only boxers for the rest of my life.) He yelled at us to get back to bed, although I think he was trying to keep a laugh hidden behind his somewhat angry expression.

We did as we were told and not fifteen minutes later, I was out there again by myself, staring at the lights. I didn't know this until much later in life, but my mom also got up to spy on me as I watched the lights by myself. She was very good, because I never caught her.

Today, I am still like a kid in my house. While I already know what Santa has brought me, I still take the time to relax on the couch and watch the twinkling lights. Only now, my two dogs and my cat usually join me—a dog on each side of me, and the cat on my lap.

DAVID LASTINGER

Tale #9: The Cooper Incident

I've had Cooper since he was an eight-week-old pup. He was the runt of his litter. The vet confirmed that his three sisters had been picking on him, by the looks of his gnawed ears. When I picked him up from the breeder, he had the cutest Mickey Mouse bandana wrapped around his little neck. Today, that same bandana would barely cover his paws. He was the happiest little fella when he was finally away from his pesky sisters. Being scooped into my arms made his stubby little tail wag like a trip hammer, all while flashing that famous Golden Retriever smile.

From the beginning, I crate-trained him, though he didn't like it very much. Often, he would howl at 3:00 a.m., so I started putting a blanket over the crate. It helped quite a bit. He was not the most popular puppy in the house when he howled or cried, but that's just part of growing up.

One night, I don't think he could take it anymore and did his best to get out. I heard a horrible screeching in the middle of the night and fell out of bed, rushing to see what the matter was. On my way to the living room, I somehow slipped on the tiled floor and landed hard on my butt. *Damn. That's gonna leave a mark.*

I pulled away the blanket to find his snout and jaw stuck between the wires of the crate. His howling was unbearable. I freed him and let him sleep on my chest for the remainder of the night.

For the next two months, he had a dent on his nose from the crate. As he got bigger, it eventually grew out.

Puppy-training school came about three months after all of his shots were done and he could join the rest of the puppies in class. Everyone liked him, including the other puppy parents. He passed with a B, though, because he couldn't sit still long enough for the trainer. There were just too many things to do and smell.

Cooper and I were also quite popular in the neighborhood. We went for a walk every morning, at first light. We always ran into at least two other dogs.

At 18 months, at fifty-five pounds, he was as big as he was going to get. In all of my life, I had never had such a small Golden. They are normally closer to eighty-five or ninety-five pounds. However, he had about a hundred pounds of character to make up for the loss in size.

One year, I had to go to a work conference that didn't allow dogs, so I ended up leaving him at one of those week-long dog camps. The place had a good reputation on all of their social media sites. I received daily updates and pictures of him playing and swimming with all of the other dogs. It sure looked like he was having a good time, despite me missing him. When I picked him up, he was happy to see me, but something seemed a little off. I wasn't able to put my finger on it. The staff said he had been great the whole time—except for once. A little dog, who thought he was a big dog, bit him on the ear. Cooper didn't like that, of course. The staff said they saw him squish the little dog with his paw and then sat on him, to bring the point home. Problem solved. They cleaned up his ear, and all seemed to be good.

Back home, he was more lethargic than normal and didn't even seem to like his best cat friend, Simon. Simon even hissed at him and escaped to the top of his cat tree. He wouldn't come down. After two days of this, things got even worse, Cooper's eyes glazed over, his coat had lost its luster, and his classic Golden smile had turned creepy and weird.

During the night, he had slipped out the doggy door for a while. In the morning, there was a pile of dead bunnies on the doorstep.

The final straw occurred the next morning when he snapped and snarled at his favorite little friend, Sally. She was a five-year-old girl who lived next door and came to see him every day. They were totally in love with each other. She ran home crying and utterly heartbroken. I took him to the vet and his bloodwork came back with disappointing results. Somehow, in that little dog bite he got, there was a zombie virus that infected Cooper. Damn those little dogs!

At that moment, I knew what I needed to do. I packed him up in his crate and drove away. When we got back to the house, I left him in the backyard. I then fetched my old .22 from the back of my closet.

It was everything I could do to level my rifle at my best friend and companion. I took sight and squeezed the trigger. All I heard was a quiet click.

"Oh, no! I can't believe that I forgot my bullets."

I ran back to the closet, grabbed a couple of bullets, and went back outside. Once I loaded the rifle, I leveled it at him again. It didn't feel any better this time. Through teary eyes, as I slowly squeezed the trigger, I was thinking that this was the worst and the best thing I have ever had to do.

Afterward, I was so distraught that I could not even go to work. My boss, also a dog lover, completely understood, because she also loved Cooper. All his friends and their parents throughout the neighborhood found out and came by to pay their respects. He had touched so many lives. Even Sally, the little girl who was his best friend, came by with her mom and a picture she had drawn for him.

After a week, I went back to work. Being in the house without Cooper made me feel even worse and I needed a decent distraction.

My co-workers did their best to be cheery around me and not bring up the Cooper incident.

After about a year, the thought of having another Golden finally crept into my head. I just can't go to the store and pick up another one, like I can with a car or a bike. They have to pick me. For me, that's just the way it is. However, I know that someday, I will be chosen again.

Tale #10: The Pesky Volunteers

Henry and Mary lived in a quiet little house just on the outskirts of Payson, Arizona. It was a second marriage for each of them, and their kids were grown and out of the house. Although they were retired, they were still active enough to take on part-time jobs to help pay for travel costs.

Just about every month, they found themselves leaving on a new adventure in their truck and travel trailer.

For an upcoming trip, they were headed to the California Redwoods. It had been on their shortlist for a while.

Finally, it was here. Henry liked the trip-planning and logistics. For him, it was part of the fun. Mary didn't like that part so much. Her job was to plan the menus and do the food prep they required.

On the Saturday morning before they were scheduled to leave, they had been scurrying around the house, getting everything ready. This time of year, there was a lot of politicking going on, due to the upcoming election. Although they always voted, they were not enthused about all of the grandstanding and baby-kissing people that came around.

Just last week, they'd heard of some overly enthusiastic volunteers entering a neighbor's home when they hadn't come to the door quickly enough. Henry felt terrible for the person. He and his neighbors would never let that happen on their street. They all looked out for one another.

That Saturday afternoon, Mary had finished her list of preparations while Henry was still out in the yard, so it was an ideal time for her to get a shower in and start relaxing. Just then, two of those nosey political ladies decided to pay them a visit. Neither Mary nor Henry heard the knock on the door or the ring of the bell. There were several doors to get through to reach the house: the gate, the screen door on the porch, and finally, the front door.

With her shower done, Mary was wrapped in just a robe with a towel around her hair when she walked into the kitchen and found two ladies there. She screamed loud enough that Henry came running in from the yard. On his way in, he grabbed one of his pistols from a hiding spot and came crashing into the kitchen. While Mary retreated to safety, Henry leveled his pistol at the two brazen ladies, who were now wide-eyed and stammering.

"What the hell are you doing in my house, and who invited you in?" he yelled at them. "Nobody did! If you were men, you'd be dead by now. Get out of my house and never come back again! And stay away from everyone else on this street. Tell your boss that he is also not welcome here."

As Henry marched the ladies out of his house, he spotted a bowl of prank snap caps that their grandkids had left behind. He grabbed a few and slammed them onto the floor right behind the intruders. The two ladies were now bent over in a sprint, despite their age, as if they could not get out the door quick enough.

Henry slammed the door shut as Mary came down the stairs. She had watched it all from the second-floor landing. They looked at each other for a moment, then burst out laughing so hard that their sides hurt.

Henry put away his pistol and called his friend, who happened to be the local sheriff. Once the sheriff was done laughing, too, he told them not to worry about a thing. He would handle any fallout that came from that political camp.

With their excitement was over for the day, Henry and Mary settled in for the night. They couldn't wait for their next adventure to begin.

Tale #11: Billy's Tree

Billy was a curious young lad who always wondered how things grew from the earth. When he was in the sixth grade, a special guest speaker from the nearby botanical gardens came to his classroom to help the children celebrate Arbor Day. She spoke of how important trees were to the community. A local tree farm even provided baby trees for Billy's entire class to plant wherever they wanted to. As part of their science class, they had to monitor and track the growth of the saplings. Each child was given a little potted tree to take home and care for.

***

I am that tree that Billy planted so many years ago. I was just a tiny oak tree at the time. Billy and his dad took great care to find just the perfect spot for me. After a week of looking, they found an opening in a grand prairie with a farm nearby and a babbling creek right next to the spot where they planted me.

I will never forget that day. Billy and his dad took turns digging the hole for my roots. They followed all of the instructions that the lady had given them and even put up a sign nearby that said "Billy's Tree."

With all of the love and attention that they gave me, it was up to me to grow as big and strong as I could for many people to enjoy my shade.

The first five years were the hardest. It was tough to stretch my roots out through the tough ground.

Like the good student he was, Billy came by to check on my growth every week. He talked to me and even brought extra water from the creek if he thought I looked thirsty.

Once in a while, Billy and his father would even bring me snacks, such as fertilizer and old coffee grounds. I was not a fan of banana peels because they were black and greasy, and took forever to break down.

The summers were my favorite part of the years. When Billy was on summer vacation, he would ride his bike over to see how I was doing. It was amazing to watch how big he was getting, too.

When I was four years old, he took the sign down and nailed it to my trunk. I guess it was getting in the way of my growing roots.

Over the years, I got bigger, as did my canopy. People from the town would come out to visit me. I've had many people take pictures of kids climbing on my strong branches. Once in a while, a kid would fall off me and break an arm or something. I didn't really like seeing that.

As each autumn arrived, I got used to seeing young couples come out to see my colors change and watch the breeze blow the leaves from my branches. By now, I had lots of names and hearts engraved in my trunk. I didn't mind because I knew this would be a special place for the couples for a long time to come.

The scariest part of the year was during the rainstorms. The thunder wasn't really a problem because it was just noise, but the lightning was terrifying. I never knew when or if it would strike me.

As I got bigger and even more robust, I grew less afraid of the lightning. Sometimes, I even laughed at it, almost daring it to strike me. Mother Nature must not have liked that.

One time, I laughed a little too hard, and she hit me with a bolt that made me lose some branches, including a critical branch—the one that held a rope swing the local kids had tied to it. I still remember the noise as the branch cracked and it and the swing crashed to the ground. Luckily, no kids were around.

Some of my grandest memories are those couples who got married under my canopy in the spring. That's when I would really shine.

Two of my favorite tree climbers were Julie and Erica. It was a pleasure to watch them grow up since they were eight years old. They had been best friends from the first day of school.

Just last year, they got married under my canopy, and the whole town came out to celebrate. It was a great party with a band and a parade. Even the Mayor said a few words for them.

The best thing of all happened just this year. Billy, a father now, brought his six-year-old son, Tommy, to visit. They began building a treehouse in me. Their father-son project is nearly done, and I can't wait for them to spend their first night in it.

Tale #12: The Coke Machine Bandits

For a few years after college, I went to work for Mack, a friend of the family. Essentially, he was the big brother I never had. He owned a vending company that provided soda machines to businesses and apartments across Phoenix. The job was actually a lot of fun, and I got to see and learn much of the Valley while working for him.

One sunny summer Saturday afternoon, I was making a delivery to an apartment complex that was not in the greatest part of town. I had been to that site numerous times, so I wasn't too worried about anything happening to me. The machine was located in the laundry room of the complex, which was also near the pool. It being summer, a bunch of kids were around, having a good time, swimming and splashing in the water.

I rolled up to the soda machine, opened its door, extracted the cash, took inventory, closed the door, and headed back to my van to get more soda. I didn't realize I had forgotten to lock the door.

On my way back to the laundry room, I noticed the pool was suddenly void of kids, although a bunch of clothing and shoes were still strewn about. Wet footprints covered the ground. They got drier the closer I got to the vending machine.

Once I got back to the machine, I understood why the pool was so quiet. Someone had discovered the machine was unlocked and the kids helped themselves to a bunch of free sodas. I was pretty mad at myself for letting my guard down, until a light went off in my head.

I calmly collected all of the shoes left at the pool and put them in my van, locked the door, and went back to stocking the machine. Two little kids came up to me and asked if they could have their shoes back.

I said, "Not until I get back every single can of soda that you and your friends stole from me." I sent the kids on their way and waited for fifteen minutes or so.

No more kids came forth, which was surprising. Nike Air Jordans were the hot shoe that year and cost about $100 a pair. I had several pairs in my van now.

Once I drove away, I called Mack to let him know what had happened. Mack could not stop laughing and said he would call the manager on Monday. The manager also laughed. She said she would contact us if any angry moms showed up in the office. Oddly enough, no one did.

We kept those shoes in our warehouse for nearly six months before donating them to a children's charity at Christmas time.

Tale #13: The Spring Dance

It was a tradition in my family that whichever kid was graduating from high school that year would also get to go to Ireland for that summer as a graduation present. My mom was born and raised there. We still have family over there.

To date, my oldest sister has been living in Ireland for about thirty years.

I was seventeen when I made the trip. My best friend, Brian, was supposed to go with me, but there were some financial complications in his family that year, which prevented him from going.

I took my bike with me and rode many miles around the country there, exploring things the best way I knew how. Riding on the wrong side of the road was weird, at first. Once I got used to it and their system of road signage, everything smoothed out.

On one excursion, I ran into the Irish military, who were out on maneuvers. For a moment, I got scared because I thought I was somewhere I wasn't supposed to be. There were giant tanks and soldiers everywhere. However, they passed by me and paid me no attention.

One crazy night, my cousin invited me to go to the local dance with him. It was a small town, and people from the other small towns nearby would also be there. I was excited at the prospect of meeting some of the local girls, even though I still had no clue about how to talk to them.

It's not a secret that American girls are crazy about Irish accents—or any foreign accent, for that matter. Being logical and naïve, I figured Irish girls would be crazy about American accents, especially those like mine, that had a Texas twang.

That evening, we got dressed up and headed over to the town hall. My cousin found a table and we hung out with all of his buddies. After the band had been playing for a bit, I spied a table of girls who looked like they were having fun.

Screwing up my courage, I walked over and asked one of the girls to dance. Oddly, she said no.

Flabbergasted, I headed back to the table to regroup.

After a while, I tried a few different tables and got the same response from the girls I asked. I could not figure out why they wouldn't dance. After all, wasn't that what they'd come for?

With no help from my cousin, I decided it was time to go home.

The house was a country mile away. It wasn't a really long walk, but it was 11 p.m., there was no moonlight, and the country roads were barely wide enough for two cars to pass without banging mirrors, so the journey was a little dicier than I had planned. However, I made it to the house safely. I was relieved to see that the lights were still on.

Oh, good. Someone's up.

I knocked on the front door a number of times. No one answered, so I went around to the back and knocked, and got the same result, oddly enough. I tried opening the doors. They were locked.

Who locks their doors in the country of a small town? Crazy.

Just then, it started to rain. I now had to find a way into the house. It was a two-story home, with no eaves to hide under. I looked for an open window, spotted one, and approached it.

The phone suddenly rang. While I tried to figure out how to climb up to the window, I heard my Aunt Mary saying that they hadn't seen me yet.

Oh, good. She was up.

I hurried around to the front door and knocked again, pretty loudly. Still no answer. *Damn it!*

The rain had changed from light droplets to a strong drizzle. The need to get inside was more pressing than ever. I saw a bathroom window open and decided that it was my best way in.

Standing on a wobbly milk can, I started clearing things from the window sill. I had just gotten my first leg and arm inside when the bathroom light came on. In Ireland, the electric power runs at 220 volts instead of 110 volts, and the light switch is outside the bathroom, not inside, like we are used to in the US.

Shit! This is not gonna end well—but it's gonna be pretty damn funny!

It was.

The only thing I could do was say, "Hi," when my Aunt Mary opened the door and exclaimed, "Jesus, Mary, and Joseph! You gave me a fright!"

I scared the crap out of her. The look on her face was priceless.

Once I was inside, we had a cup of tea and some biscuits—cookies, to Americans—while I told her the story. She had not laughed about anything that hard in a long time.

Tired from the whole ordeal, we both went to bed.

The next morning, my uncle tried to have some sort of serious talk with me. I have no idea what he actually said. I wasn't really paying attention. I think it was some sort of uncle-type talk about guys and gals. Shortly after that, I got up and went for a long ride, which usually clears things up for me.

For the record, I skipped the next two dances.

Tale #14: The Treehouse Proposal

Jimmy and Lauren were having their usual breakfast at their favorite coffee house in town. Jimmy normally had a full breakfast of eggs, bacon, toast, and hash browns. Today, however, he was having only toast and coffee.

"Aren't you hungry, Jimmy?" Lauren asked, noticing his smaller breakfast. "What's wrong?"

"Ah, nothing wrong at all. I just didn't feel like eating a bunch today."

He hoped that he had convinced her that everything was okay. In fact, he was hoping everything would be more than okay—and maybe even life-changing—by the end of the day.

They had been dating for almost a year now and everything had been going very well. Somehow, he knew deep down inside that Lauren was the girl for him for the rest of his life.

He could not believe that he was going to try marriage again. After being stood up at the altar by Amy two years ago, he didn't think this day would ever come. When Amy rejected him, he was shocked, embarrassed, and didn't know how to explain it to his friends and family. Even though he was out the money, that loss wasn't nearly as devastating as the event itself. What made it worse was that there were no warning or red flags, so he couldn't even have predicted that from her. He never saw it coming. Lauren, on the other hand, was proving to be quite different.

Jimmy was a handyman and had developed a nice-sized clientele in the town where he and his dad lived. He never felt like he belonged in college. Nothing appealed to him, as far as a career went. Fixing things and using his hands appealed to him most. His favorite classes in school were wood and metal shop.

Lauren had just relocated to town and into a house that she inherited from her favorite uncle. As a kid, she had been to the house many times, and had fallen in love with it over the years. It was old and certainly needed its share of updates and repairs. As a civil engineer with a minor in interior design, she knew what she wanted to do to the house but didn't have the time to do it.

Lauren looked for a handyman to help her. After trying a few who disappointed her, she stumbled across Jimmy's website. She checked him out thoroughly before she called him to talk about her home.

"Classic Handyman Service. This is Jimmy."

"Hi, Jimmy. My name is Lauren Perry and I think I need your help."

She went on to explain about her uncle's house, its sticking doors, and the creaky sounds from the water heater.

"When can you come out for a look?"

"Hi, Lauren. I think I know which house you are in. Would tomorrow at three work for you?"

"Yes. Thank you. See you then!"

As Jimmy hung up the phone, he realized that something about her voice had registered with him for no apparent reason. He wasn't sure what it was but would find out tomorrow.

The next day, he rang the doorbell. Within a moment, a woman opened the door. The first thing he noticed was her beautiful red hair and the freckles on her face. They locked eyes for just a moment when Jimmy turned away.

Upon opening the door, she also stopped. He was tall and had blond, rumpled hair. She couldn't pull away from his blue eyes fast enough to not get caught staring. It was too late; the sparks had already started. He caught himself and put out his hand to her.

"Hi, I'm Jimmy. You must be Lauren."

"Yes. Thanks for coming out. The last couple of guys that I had booked no-showed me. Bastards!"

Jimmy laughed because it was not the first time he had heard that. Poor bastards. They were missing out on business and a good-looking client.

Over the summer, he found himself at her house quite often, not only fixing things but also having great conversations. Sometimes, he would even forget what he had come there to fix. He didn't complain, and neither did she.

After they had their first date and she kissed him at the end of it, he knew he was going to be hooked for life.

Jimmy had just finished working on a passion project for one of his best clients. He took on such projects once in a while, when his job schedule lightened up a little. This project, in particular, involved building a huge treehouse on the client's ranch just outside of town. He got excited, just like a kid at Christmas, when the idea was presented to him. As a child, Jimmy had always wanted a treehouse, but his family lived in an apartment, so it just wasn't logical.

Lauren had been especially helpful in the beginning stages of the treehouse project. She was a civil engineer with a background in interior design. She had been out to the treehouse a few times, in the early stages of the build.

Due to her busy schedule, she had not yet seen the completed project.

What Lauren didn't know was that he planned to propose to her this very afternoon at the treehouse.

"How do you feel about an early dinner, around five?" Jimmy asked, drinking the last of his coffee.

"Sure, that sounds great. It's been a crazy week and I don't feel like staying out all night." Lauren sounded a little more tired than usual.

"Great. I'll swing by your place around four-thirty. Oh, yeah, bring your sneakers!" Jimmy said with a wry smile and a twinkly eye, getting up to leave.

"What? Why?"

"Just trust me. Now, I have to get rolling. I have a ton of work to do today before dinner." With that, he left the diner, jumped in his truck, and sped away.

Jimmy was always doing something to surprise Lauren. He loved to see the look on her face when she got her surprise. It was one of the things that made him fall in love with her so quickly.

Lauren didn't initially put much thought into his instructions. She was used to him pulling little stunts and surprises. As the day wore on, she began to think about things a little more. It was curious that Jimmy only had a light breakfast. Now, she was beginning to wonder what he was up to, and what she would need sneakers for.

Jimmy had a lot of work to do before their dinner date. A few days prior, he had talked to Lauren's girlfriend about what kind of ring she might like. Lisa was only too happy to help out, as she loved both of them and could not have been more excited. They went to a neighboring city so

Lauren wouldn't see them in town. Her office was downtown and just across the street from the jewelry store.

He had also asked his clients with the treehouse if he could propose there. They were thrilled to be included on his special day and happy to help in any way they could.

It was their job to quietly gather his friends and family and have them waiting in the barn for the high sign that she said yes.

Joe Harper was Jimmy's dad and probably the most excited of everyone. He loved Lauren right from the first time they met and had a feeling this would happen. It wasn't often that Jimmy brought home a girl to meet him. Joe reminisced a little, as he was sad for his wife, Emma. She had died just a few years earlier. Lauren was the kind of girl that she would have loved.

Last week, Jimmy had told Joe about his plans.

"Dad, I am thinking of asking Lauren to marry me. What do you think?"

"Really? Oh, my goodness. That's wonderful! What took you so long to get here? I knew this would happen six months ago." Joe could not hide the smile on his face or the delight in his eyes. "Do you have a ring yet?

"Not yet, but Lisa and I went into town last week to pick something out. She has great taste and will help me get something just right for Lauren."

The treehouse itself was a work of art. The owners had given him a list of must-haves and left the rest for him and Lauren to design. It was built 20 feet up, between a few trees. It had a grand, winding staircase around one of the trunks, which led up to a large, wooden deck with railings. Planters full of roses lined the deck. The desk also contained a gas fireplace surrounded by comfy chairs just right for enjoying the peace and quiet on the ranch. The light inside the great room came through a wall of windows on both the east and west sides. The treehouse was going to be a wonderful place to catch the sunrises and sunsets that their part of the country was known for.

One of Jimmy's woodworking masterpieces in the house was a hidden bedroom and bathroom. If you knew just which book to pull on the shelf, you could open the secret door. Not even Lauren knew about this little detail.

At 4:00 p.m., it was time to put his plan into action. Jimmy checked in with everyone. They were all in their places. The ring was tucked safely in the secret bedroom so that he wouldn't accidentally lose it.

He hurried back home with just enough time to shower and clean up.

Patti was another close friend of Lauren's who was in on the plan, too. Her job was to steal Lauren away for a girl's day at the spa. Both of them were looking forward to it and catching up on girl talk.

Jimmy rolled up to Lauren's house right at 4:30. Being punctual was something that she could count on Jimmy for.

He knocked on the door while hiding a bunch of flowers behind his back.

"Wow, Jimmy, you look so handsome." It was hard to hide her smile whenever she saw him.

"Why, thank you." He pulled the flowers from behind his back. "These are for you."

Her surprised look was soon followed by a frown.

"Uh-oh, what did you do now, Jimmy?" Lauren asked.

"N-n-nothing. Really, I just saw these flowers and they were calling your name."

"Oh, nice recovery, Jimmy!" Lauren said with a smile that let him off the hook. She could get him every time with that and it never got old. "Where are we going? I don't think I am dressed up enough for this."

"Believe me, Lauren, you look wonderful. I can't tell you. You will just have to trust me. I am certain that you will love this place."

About halfway to the ranch, Jimmy told her that she would have to wear a blindfold for the last mile or so. It was all part of the surprise. Lauren was game for just about anything, which was another thing that he loved so much about her.

She was always supportive of his dreams, too. In the past, others were not, so Jimmy felt like she believed in him. She also laughed at his jokes.

He pulled over and handed her the blindfold.

Once it was on, he checked to make sure she couldn't see. He knew she would try to peek just a little bit. She began asking lots of questions, trying to get him to spill the beans. Jimmy smiled so hard and was happy that she couldn't see him.

"Jimmy, this is killing me! What's going on? If you tell me now, I will go topless for the rest of the trip!"

Although he was tempted, he held fast and didn't take the bait.

Before Jimmy finished the blindfolded part of the drive, he stopped to text Patti that they were around the corner and ask if everything was set up. The short pause added to Lauren's anxiousness to find out what he was up to. Patti had successfully gotten everyone hidden in the barn. It would spoil the surprise if Lauren caught sight of anyone. They had glasses and bottles of champagne ready to pop if she said yes.

Jimmy rolled up to the base of the tree and came around her side to help Lauren out of his truck. He took her arm and guided her up the perfectly laid stone pathway.

"Okay, I got you now. Watch your step. You're doing great, just a little bit more. Okay, stop!

What I am about to show you will change your life. Are you ready for this Lauren Perry?"

"Yes, yes, yes!" The excitement in her voice now could not be hidden.

"One, two, two-and-a-half—" He tried to stretch it out as much as he could. "Three!" He pulled off the blindfold with one quick movement and let it drop to the ground.

As Lauren took in her first look at the completed treehouse, she was speechless and started to cry.

"Oh, my God, Jimmy, this is beautiful," she said, between sniffs. He handed her a tissue.

"There's more! Follow me upstairs."

The smell of the trees and fresh air filled her senses as they made their way up the grand staircase, up to the patio deck with chairs and roses everywhere. She could smell the fresh-cut lumber. It was a smell that always made her happy.

As Lauren looked around in earnest, she saw some of her designs and plans in place. She let out an "Ooh" each time she discovered another beautiful detail.

She stopped when she got to the bookcase that covered a large section of the room. For some reason, it just seemed out of place.

"There is another surprise for you." Jimmy smiled.

"What? I don't think I can take any more surprises. This is fabulous!"

"Reach in the bookcase and get me the copy of *Gone with the Wind*." It was one of her favorite books of all time.

She found it and tugged at it. As she pulled on it, she heard a series of clicks. A worried look crossed her face and she jumped back a little bit. The bookcase slowly slid back into itself to reveal the hidden bedroom.

She squealed with surprise.

"What? No way, a hidden room! This is the coolest thing ever!"

She entered it, awestruck. While she was looking around, Jimmy retrieved the ring from its hiding spot and slipped it into his pocket.

The sun was starting to set outside and had turned the sky a million colors of red and blue. She went to a window and took in the view.

Then, she turned around to face Jimmy.

"You have outdone yourself! You should be very proud. I know that I am."

She gave him a big kiss.

He took her hand and led her over to the handmade railing fashioned from branches found nearby. He faced her, then put his hands around her shoulders.

"Lauren, from the day I met you, I never stopped thinking about you, your laugh, your eyes, and how hard you hit me when I tell a bad joke."

She put her hand over her mouth and giggled.

He got down on his knee and withdrew a little red box from his pocket.

"You are the best thing that has ever happened to me and I want to make you as happy as you have made me. Lauren Perry, will you marry me?"

He looked up into her eyes. They filled with tears. She was speechless. She couldn't tell anyone, but she had been waiting for this moment from the first day she met him, too.

"Oh, yes! I would be happy to marry you!"

The ring slid onto her finger like it was made for her. He stood up and she kissed him for what seemed like forever.

Meanwhile, their friends and family had gathered quietly at the base of the tree, champagne glasses in hand.

Just when Jimmy knew they were all there, he leaned over the railing as if he was talking to the trees and shouted, "She said yes!"

Lauren was taken aback one more time as champagne corks started popping and a cheer came up from the crowd below. Lauren smiled at her friends and looked at Jimmy with a gleam in her eye as she playfully punched him in the arm one more time. Again, she was speechless and happy.

DAVID LASTINGER

Tale #15: A Midnight Swing

The full moon was shining brightly. It lit up the lake so well that Johnny would not need the flashlight that he brought with him. It was nearly midnight and so many thoughts were running through his head that sleep was not an option.

Tomorrow would be his first day at the new school. He was nervous about making new friends because he wasn't very good at it. Would the other students laugh at him, or even worse, not even talk to him? What about his teacher? No one could measure up to the favorite one that he had to leave behind. What if she didn't like him, or what if he didn't like her? What if they served icky food for lunch and he had to go hungry?

There were so many worries for a fifth-grader.

Johnny and his family had moved during the summer. Their new house was much bigger than the one they left behind. It even had a lake with its own boat ramp and dock.

Next to the lake was a giant, old oak tree. It had many branches, including one most important one, which stretched out over the lake and had a rope swing attached to it. The rope even had the right number of knots on it for getting a better grip. It had been left behind by the previous owner because his kids had outgrown it and moved to the city. Johnny could swing for what seemed like hours or until his mom rang the dinner bell. When he was swinging, he felt free and all of his troubles seemed to fade away.

Tonight was no exception. He sneaked out his bedroom window and headed for the lake. Just like he had seen on a recent TV show, he arranged his pillows and blankets to look like he was still in bed. He knew that his mom would check in on him before she went to bed. His plan was to be back in bed before she found out.

As he walked down the gravel pathway, he could hear all of the lake's night life. Crickets were singing, an old bullfrog was croaking at the water's edge, and a lonesome coyote was howling from across the water.

The light from the moon was casting curious shadows as it poured through the tree's leaves.

Earlier that day, Johnny had stashed a small backpack under a nearby bush. In it was a change of clothes, a towel from the bathroom, a tiny can of orange soda, and a granola bar. He looked around while he waited to make sure the coast was clear. He certainly didn't want anyone to find out. This was his private time, and although he didn't exactly understand why, it was important to him. Carefully, he approached the swing, still looking around to make sure no one else came. The coast was clear.

Higher and higher he swung as the night breeze gave him a slight chill. This was his favorite time. It was also when he felt the most alive. As he slowed to a stop and jumped back onto the beach, he saw what looked like a little girl about his age. He hadn't seen her walk up. He thought he was there all alone. Oddly enough, he was not scared. She approached him, said hi, and asked if she could swing. Not knowing what to think, he handed her the rope and went to sit on the dock.

After she had swung for a while, she jumped off. A moment later, she sat down beside Johnny and introduced herself.

"I'm Caitlin. I live over there." She pointed to a neighboring house.

He found out that she went to the school he was also going to, so he took this chance to ask her about the school, the teacher, and even the cafeteria food. She said the teacher is nice, and most of the kids are okay. She finished up by saying the food was all right, but it was best to bring your own lunch on Mondays.

With all of his troubles swung away and his important life questions answered, it was time to sneak back into the house. Just like a ninja, he stealthily scaled the side of the house, climbed through his bedroom window, and successfully got back in bed without his mom noticing. All was right with the world.

Johnny went to his first day of class the next morning and came away with a nice teacher as well as a great new friend and neighbor.

Tale #16: Jimmy and the Gas-Pump Karen

Jimmy had just gotten home from a tough day at work on a customer's house. Their custom closet project had some snags he had yet to figure out, but for today, he was done. He was looking forward to "beer o'clock," kicking off his boots, and relaxing with Lauren.

"Hey, sweetie, I'm home. Where are you?" Jimmy hollered as he strolled through the front door.

"I'm in the library," Lauren yelled back.

She had sprained her ankle last week by awkwardly stepping off a curb. He found her resting in a chair with her leg up and an ice pack on her ankle.

"Hi, you studly man. How was your day?" She winked as he bent over to give her a kiss.

"I'll spare you the details, but sometimes old houses and measurements don't quite mix," he said with a grimace. "I'm headed for a beer. Want one?"

"No, thanks."

Jimmy had just exited the room when Lauren called out to him in her sexiest voice.

"Hey, babe, before you get changed and settled in, can I ask you a favor?"

He stopped, rolled his eyes, and wondered what sort of wild thing she was going to say now. Geez, she could have texted me while I was on my way home. I was going right past the store.

He popped his head back through the door and put his best smile on.

"Sure, what's up?"

"I'm sorry to ask because I'd rather do it myself, ya know. My car needs gas, and I'm leaving early in the morning to attend that conference in Flagstaff. Would you mind gassing it up for me?" She winked and playfully tugged on her robe. "I'll make it worth your while, studly man!"

Oh, well. How could he say no to that? Or anything that she asks, for that matter?

So, off to the gas station, he went.

Once he arrived, the station looked really busy, and three of the gas pumps were down for service. That was not helping the crowd at all.

After circling the pumps several times to find a spot, he finally saw one and dove in—or tried to. Halfway there, a lady in a fancy car spied the same spot and also tried to dive in. Now, they were bumper to bumper, and yet still so far away from getting their gas.

The lady threw up her hands and started yelling something that Jimmy couldn't understand. He stood his ground and shook his head no at her.

This was his pump, and he wasn't giving it up without a fight.

The lady had some sort of frizzy hairstyle set off with a fashionable headband that could have been from the '70s. She rolled down her window and continued to yell.

"Are you serious right now? This is my pump. I saw it first."

Jimmy remained calm. He still had his window up and continued to shake his head "No" at her.

She finally got out of her car and stood between her car and its door. Jimmy rolled down his window to hear her story.

"This is my spot. I saw it first."

"I'm sorry, Ma'am, but I was here first."

"Are you serious? Oh, my God! No, you were not!"

Leaning his head out the window, Jimmy affirmed, "Yes, Ma'am, I was."

"Well, this isn't my regular car, so you have to let me in."

Jimmy busted out laughing and said, "Well, this isn't my regular car, either. What does that have to do with anything?"

By now, there was a bit of a crowd, and people were starting to watch this "Karen" drama unfold. Some snickers could be heard at Jimmy's retort.

She continued making a scene.

"Well, I already paid for this pump," she argued.

On a typical day, Jimmy would have been in his work truck and would have conceded the spot. Everyone has a camera these days, and he didn't need any negative publicity. However, he was tired, hungry, and 15 minutes away from getting some nooky, so he was not giving his spot up.

"Ma'am, there is no way you paid cash for this spot. If you had, you would have already been parked here. I doubt you pay cash for anything. Now, move your car!" His voice got a little louder as he got more annoyed.

She just stood there with her arms folded across her chest, like she wasn't about to move.

"Darling, we are both in a hurry, but I have all day to wait if you are going to be this rude. You are also causing a scene. Back up and find another spot." By now, Jimmy had stepped out of his wife's tiny car and stood up to his full six-foot-four height.

Just then, the store manager came up to the woman. She had seen the event unfold and approached the gas-pump "Karen."

"Ma'am, this gentleman was here first. You need to find another spot. You are holding up my customers, and they also have important things to do today."

"Well, I wanna speak to your manager," she demanded, hands on her hips.

"Okay, talk. I am the manager," she smiled. "I say, move your car now, or I will have the police do it for you. As a matter of fact, they are already on their way here."

The poor lady finally realized that she wouldn't get her way and got back in her car. She gunned the engine and threw it in reverse. She squealed her tires as a police officer approached. He was just in time to see her crash into a parked car in front of the store.

The officer walked over to her car, pulled her out, and put her in handcuffs. Jimmy smiled as a cheer went up from the crowd. As it turns out, this "Karen" had several warrants out for her arrest for various parking violations and a DUI charge.

Jimmy calmly filled up his wife's car. He tipped his hat to the lady and said, "God bless you. I will pray for you." Then, he rolled away with a big smile on his face.

Tale #17: A Day in the Life of 47

At 4:30 a.m., Tony's alarm clock went off. He was not used to getting up this early, and he had forgotten to wash his uniforms in the laundry the night before. It was part of his routine but his girlfriend's birthday party was last night, and he stayed up way too late. He quickly sorted just a few sets and started the washing machine.

While he was waiting for that to finish, he pulled out his laptop to check on his social media pages. Then, he made his lunch.

With his lunch bag in hand and fresh laundry on his back, he headed out for his car. Unfortunately, the haunting sound of the "click, click, click" from the starter told him his battery was dead.

"Barnacles!" This was not the way he wanted to start his week.

His neighbor was usually up early, and luckily, he answered the door when Tony knocked.

"Hey, Bill! I'm sorry to bother you, but can you give me a jump? My damn battery is acting up."

"Of course, man."

Within a few minutes, they had Tony's car running again.

He jumped in and headed for the plant after calling them to let them know he was on his way.

He was a good employee and hated to be late. The boss understood, but Tony felt terrible about it anyway.

Because he arrived late this morning, he did not get his favorite delivery truck. All the drivers there had a favorite, and it was first come, first serve. Tony delivered custom medical instruments and equipment to local hospitals and doctors' offices. He had gotten used to "his" truck, and driving something different was something he was not looking forward to, especially with the way his day started and the busy day in front of him.

So, it was Truck 47 that he ended up with—a gutless wonder of American engineering that was supposed to be reliable and gas-efficient. Nobody really liked it, and it was usually pawned off on the rookies. It was also loud, goofy-looking, and had a crappy radio.

Tony walked out to his vehicle for the day.

"Hey, 47, how are you doing today?"

"Oh, Tony, it's you! I'm glad it's you because that new guy yesterday was a hot mess of a driver."

Tony snickered, "Really? How so?"

"He sits in me like no professional driver would. His seat was all the way back, at a weird angle, and his arms stretched out straight, like he was a robot. I know I am not the biggest or coolest motor vehicle out there, but if you treat me nicely, I can get you there in one piece. I think he was trying to keep up with some tuner truck yesterday. He's kinda dumb."

Tony looked at his truck with a concerned look on his face. "Okay, let me get you dialed in, and then we can hit the road. I will be right back."

"Okay, but it's Tuesday, and I'd rather just sit here. Besides, I've got a weird spot on my tire, there are three cracks in my windshield, and for some reason, my oil feels heavy."

"Damn, 47! Would you stop whining? You're not gonna be like this all day, are you?"

"Sorry, Tony. I know I shouldn't complain. At least, I have a job and am not sitting around like some of the trucks I know. I should be grateful. This Covid thing has really taken the air out of some of their tires."

Tony smiled at 47. "Now, that's more like it. Okay, let's get rolling. We have a lot to do today."

Truck 47 complained again. "Oh, no, I hate the freeway! Do we have to go that way again? Last time, there was this dump truck that nearly swallowed me whole. My little motor just can't compete. I can barely get out of my own shadow."

Tony patted his dash in an assuring kind of way. "Yeah, I know. Getting you on the freeway is scary for me, too, but it's the best way to get to where we are going on time. Otherwise, this would take more than all day."

With a heavy sigh, 47 gave in. "Fine, if you must, but don't flog me like that guy did yesterday. He was mean to me, and he called me bad names. He even compared me to a Chevy!"

"I will do what I can but can't promise anything. Traffic is what it is, and we just have to adapt. If I can get a good, long run on the ramp, I won't have to mash your pedal."

On a hope and a prayer, 47 blinked his eyes, quickly cleaned his windshield, and got ready to hit the freeway. Tony pressed the gas pedal and waited for the five-second lag in response—not turbo lag, just lag. They got lucky and found a nice hole in the traffic—with no dump trucks around.

47 chimed in again as Tony started tuning in the radio.

"That guy yesterday was listening to some radio talk show and yelling back at it like it could hear him. He was mad as a wet hen about something at the zoo and some argument between the elephants and the donkeys. Crazy humans. I'm so glad you listen to music. Oh, one request, if I may be so bold, no country, please."

Thankfully, they made it to the first stop with no other drama. As they pulled into the dock, 47 saw one of his friends and gave him a quick beep on the horn. His buddy beeped back and flashed his lights at him, kinda like the bro nod.

He was thankful that Tony unloaded the heaviest boxes first. Maybe this will drop his lag down to three seconds instead of five. Tony was back before he even had a chance to cool down, and they were off to the second stop.

At the traffic light, he saw an older car next to him. It was shiny, with chrome everywhere. However, there seemed to be something wrong with him because he was booming and vibrating so much it was making 47's wipers chatter. His springs must have been shot as well because he was lower to the ground than a speed bump. Truck 47 was happy when the light turned green again.

It was typical morning work traffic with all sorts of vehicles on the road. They all seemed to be in a bigger hurry than 47 was. Tony told 47 that his boss monitors how he drives, so he couldn't act like an idiot driver. Besides, Tony prided himself on being a professional driver and tried to set an example on the road.

At their next stop, they parked next to a yellow Mini.

47 got a little shy around cute girls, but he managed to say hi anyway.

"Good morning. How are you?"

The Mini looked over at him. "Oh, hi. I'm just fine. I didn't hear you come in."

47 smiled back at her and asked, "Did you see that pothole over there?"

Mini laughed and said, "Yeah, it's a big one. I'm glad my driver just missed it. Those things make me rattle like crazy! Oh, my driver is back. I gotta go now. Watch out for those potholes!" With that, she drove off with a beep and a blink of her eyes at him. He beeped back and watched her drive away. She was cute and had nice taillights, too.

Tony came back and got in the seat. "You were flirting with that Mini, weren't you? Damn, 47, you are such a player!"

"Who, me? No way. I am just friendly and work for a living" 47 retorted in his best humble voice.

Tony rolled his eyes. "Yeah, right!"

A few deliveries later, they ended up at a hospital. 47 got excited now because there was a helicopter on the pad next to where they parked. 47 loves helicopters and sometimes wished he was one of them.

He beeped at the helicopter. "Hey, Robinson, how are ya doing? Going anywhere soon?"

"Hey, 47, I haven't seen you in a while. You are looking good. I just heard my radio crackle something about leaving soon. You're gonna want to roll up your windows for this one. It's gonna get windy." Robinson laughed. Helicopter humor, ya know.

Sure enough, the crew ran out to the chopper and started it up. 47 loved this part the best—when that turbine engine starts up.

Whirrrrrrr-whiiiine-boosh! The rotors turned even faster. Undoubtedly, it was a lot windier now. Robinson lifted up, did a spin, and headed off to go rescue someone.

For both 47 and Tony, this was the highlight of the day and their last stop—a great way to wrap it up, for sure. On the way back to the plant, Tony stopped to refuel.

As a treat for 47, he squeegeed the front and back windows.

"Thanks, Tony. That was really nice. They were getting really buggy!"

"No problem. It was fun driving with you today!"

Tony pulled into a shady spot on the lot and unloaded him.

"47, you take the rest of the day off, and I will see you tomorrow. Good work today! Now, I have to go see about a new battery for my car. I sure hope she starts."

Tale #18: The Best Road Trip Ever

It was Friday morning when Greg and Sophie got the dreaded news from their doctor. It finally explained the horrendous headaches and fainting spells that Greg had been having for the past year. They were hoping for something that would be easily fixable, maybe with a pill, so everyone could go back to their normal lives. Unfortunately, fate had something different in mind.

A tumor had been growing in Greg's brain. In non-medical jargon, Dr. Collins explained that it was inoperable. At best, Greg had four months to live. They only had a few options. One was a very risky surgery that could kill Greg right on the table. Another was to try chemotherapy, which Greg refused. The last choice the doctor offered was to do nothing at all and see what happens.

"Okay, Doc, if I am hearing you right, I only have these three choices," Greg said.

Dr. Collins nodded his head in agreement from the other side of his desk.

"Yep, that's it, in a nutshell. It's a big deal and a lot to swallow at one time. Take the next week to think about it. I will see you here again, next Friday."

Greg and Sophie left the doctor's office and called their only son, Andy, to meet them for breakfast.

"What did the doctor say?" Andy queried.

"It's too important to tell you on the phone. Meet us at our usual breakfast place and we will fill you in."

Andy's boss was not happy that his best employee had to leave for part of the day. Andy liked his job well enough, and it paid the bills, yet he knew that it wasn't what he wanted to do for the rest of his life.

Thirty minutes later, the three were seated in a booth. Mimosas were served all around.

Sophie sat quietly with weepy eyes and emitted a sobbing sniffle every now and then. Andy listened closely as Greg told him what the doctor had said. After he was done, Andy sat silently for a few minutes, processing the news that he had just received.

"Will it hurt if you don't do anything?" asked Andy.

"As it gets worse, yes, but with drugs, I can manage the pain and dizziness. I have no interest in chemotherapy, and the surgery could kill me immediately. Son, I have played it safe my whole life. I was always too afraid to lose what I had worked so hard for. I think it's time your Pop had some fun."

Again, Andy was silent for a few minutes. He drained his mimosa. Finally, he looked up with a big grin on his face and a gleam in his eye.

Greg and Sophie looked at him like he had gone mad.

He explained, "Dad, I am so sorry for the grin, but I have the best idea of all time. Hear me out."

It was Greg and Sophie's turn to listen as Andy spelled out his idea.

"Dad, you have always wanted to take an epic road trip, but we never got around to it. There was always something that stopped us, usually money. Now would be the perfect time to do this."

As his parents began picking up on his idea, all of a sudden, the pain and worry disappeared from their faces. Greg grinned. Even Sophie lightened up enough and allowed a little smile to come across her face.

"Dad, we both love sports car racing, and I think there is a list of tracks we need to go see!"

"Holy crap, son, that would be awesome! I already have a shortlist in my head, but what vehicle are we going to use? Both of our cars kinda suck for this sort of thing."

Greg laughed.

"We will buy a truck and a camper. The drive will be great, and we can go as fast or as slow as we want to. There are loads of national forest campgrounds along the way, and we can stay there for a lot cheaper than at a motel or hotel."

Sophie pitched in, "I have an uncle that is not using his dually truck right now. Maybe he will let you use that. I'll call him today."

"Dad, this means we get to go camper shopping. Get the bill. Let's go!" Andy could barely contain his excitement.

The rest of the week flew by as they shopped for and bought a camper.

Soon, it was Friday morning again. Dr. Collins walked into his office, expecting to see somber faces, but was greeted by smiles instead. He figured something was up. As the couple explained their road trip plan to him, he was immediately on board and wished he could go with them.

The doctor would lay out care instructions and the necessary drugs to make the trip possible. He would also arrange for Greg to have a checkup about halfway through the trip.

When they left the office, Greg and Sophie had another surprise for Andy.

"The trip is already paid for! Your mom and I have discussed that she will get my life insurance policy when I go, so I am going to blow as much of my 401(k) as possible. Son, I can't take it with me, so if we are gonna do this, let's do it right!"

It took the next three weeks of planning and learning how their new camper worked before the guys felt ready to hit the road. Sophie was going to stay home. The plan was for the men to go to as many racetracks as possible and stay at campgrounds along the way. They also decided that they would follow one of their favorite race teams on the circuit, Clippity Clop Racing. They were an underdog team and always fun to watch.

The first stop on their journey from San Diego was Willow Springs. Located near Lancaster, it was an easy drive and allowed them to get used to how things worked. Greg volunteered to drive first, for as much of the trip as possible. Andy would take over when necessary.

As they rolled through the racetrack gates on Saturday morning, they were greeted by the lovely sounds of a V8 engine at full song coming down the straightaway. As luck would have it, their camping spot was located in a prime spot to see most of the track.

Donning their ear gear and pit passes, they practically ran to the paddocks to get a closer look at their team. The day passed quickly. Soon they were back in their camper, with Greg dreaming of driving his own racecar as they faded off to sleep.

In the morning, they headed down to the track for the final race. Clippity Clop came in third place! It was a fantastic run for them.

They broke camp, then headed for the Pacific Coast Highway and their next stop on the trip, Big Sur. It was a beautiful drive. With the windows open, they could hear waves crashing on the beaches and smell the fresh, salty air.

Greg's headaches had not really started yet, so he was still feeling good. They spent all day at the beach. Later on, the sounds of the ocean rocked them to sleep.

The next morning, they began making their way to the next racetrack, Laguna Seca. They were about halfway there when Greg pulled over and asked Andy to drive.

"My head is killing me and it's getting hard to drive. I'm gonna take a pill and rest for a bit."

There was a truck stop nearby, so they pulled in to gas up and switch places. Andy went inside to get coffee and some snacks. Soon, they were back on the road, with Andy at the wheel.

A little while later, Andy pulled into their camp spot at the track. Greg woke up from his nap.

"Damn, son, how fast did you drive? I just went to sleep fifteen minutes ago."

"Dad, it was more like two hours ago, and you needed the sleep. Oh, yeah, by the way, you snore." They both laughed. Greg never believed it when Sophie would complain about it.

"I'm feeling better now, and can tell things are changing in my head. The drugs that Doc gave me are working pretty well, so far. You get things set up, and I'll start cooking dinner."

Before they went to bed, Sophie called to check in on her boys.

"I hope you are having a blast. I was thinking that you might want to start one of those vlog things we keep hearing about. It could be fun to see how many people will tune in to watch."

Andy took a few minutes to explain to his dad what a vlog was and how it worked. Greg was on board because it sounded like fun. Before they went to bed, they recorded their first session and posted it.

In the morning, they took a golf cart ride into the paddock area where their team was setting up for the day. Laguna Seca was a famous racetrack, mostly for its Corkscrew turn. The tricky, downhill turn made for exciting racing.

The crew chief saw them arrive and pulled them aside for a minute.

"I heard about you two from my social media manager. He showed us your video from last night. We are honored that you have chosen to follow us. With that, the boys and I have decided to make you honorary team members for the rest of the year."

He pulled a pair of race credentials and two team jerseys out from behind his back that already had their names on them.

The noise from the cars was starting to get to Greg and his headaches, so he doubled up on the earplugs and noise-cancelling headphones, which made such a difference that he was able to hang out for the rest of the race.

On the way back to their campsite, Greg opened up to Andy a little bit,

"Son, this trip has, by far, been the coolest thing I have ever done, and I am happy that you are here for it. I regret not spending more time with you when you were growing up. Your mama did a fine job of raising you into a good man. I just want to say that I am proud of you."

"Thanks, Dad. I would have not missed this for anything. This will be something I will remember for a long time."

They hit the road and headed for Sonoma and the third race of the season. It wasn't a good weekend for Clippity Clop because their driver crashed about halfway through the race. He was okay, but the car was a mess. Their team was going to be out for a few races while they got busy on repairs.

While they were in the pits, their chief asked Andy if his dad had ever been in a racecar.

"No, but he has always wanted to. Why?"

"Just curious." The chief winked.

"We are going to be on the road for a bit, going through a lot of the national forests and cities we have never been to. Will you be ready by Road Atlanta?"

The chief said, "Yes. We will be looking forward to seeing you two there."

Their next stop was the California Redwoods. It was so quiet there that Greg was able to take out his earplugs and just listen to the sounds of the woods. He found himself sitting on a fallen log and reflecting on all that had happened thus far. He had made some mistakes in his life, but he had nothing to complain about.

Their next stop was Portland, Oregon. They did their part to keep it weird by taking the city ghost tour and making a stop at a crazy donut shop.

Seattle was next on their list of cities to visit. After spending the morning downtown, Greg ran out of energy and needed a nap. Andy was getting pretty good at reading his father's energy levels and quitting before he zonked out completely.

Yellowstone and the Grand Teton National Park were their next stops. They were planning to spend a few days at the parks, so they opted for a hotel room instead of the camper for a break. The big beds and fancy shower were really nice.

In the meantime, they were still posting their daily vlogs. What they didn't plan on was that they were going viral and people wanted to meet them. Much to their surprise, they were getting requests for interviews with TV and radio stations.

Greg didn't want to partake in anything just yet.

"Let's table everything until we get to Denver. We have an appointment there with a colleague of Dr. Collins to give me a checkup," Greg told Andy.

Yellowstone was certainly living up to their expectations. They saw plenty of wildlife and even got lucky enough to see a bear.

Old Faithful, the cone geyser in Yellowstone National Park, even spouted right on time, which they got on camera for their vlog.

As planned, they made their way to Denver and met with the doctor. Of course, the tumor was getting bigger but slower than the rate they had anticipated. They had all agreed at the start of the trip that once it got to a particular size, they would stop and head for home.

At dinner that night, they were discussing what the doctor had said and where they were on their trip.

Greg said, "I can feel myself slowing down a little bit, but I am still having a blast. I really want to see Road America before this is all over. If we have to skip a stop or two, I am fine with that. I got an email from the Clippity Clop chief and he said they would be at Road America for sure and waiting for us."

"Okay, Dad, that sounds like a plan. I've been keeping an eye on you. You make the call. It's your trip. What do you want to do next?"

"Let's skip Dallas and head right for Austin. I want to get some barbecue at Smokey Mo's, and maybe even go see a show at the Austin City Limits Music Festival."

That morning, as they were preparing to head out of town, they accepted an interview with one of the local TV stations. The reporter and crew were great fun and made them feel comfortable, despite them being nervous about being on TV for the first time. The crew said the story would run on the national news that night.

When they arrived in Austin, they again voted for a hotel. It was time for another break from the tiny beds and meager shower in the camper.

While they had been driving, Andy had called ahead to the Austin City Limits Music Festival staff to book tickets for that night's show. One of Greg's favorite blues singers was performing. The staff said they had seen their broadcast and had a surprise waiting for them when they show up to the "Will Call" window.

Early in the morning, they drove down to Smokey Mo's BBQ to get in line. Getting there early was essential because the restaurant usually ran out of stuff quickly. They found a spot in the back of the parking lot that would fit their dually.

They were just about to get out of their truck when they were approached by a guy wearing a T-shirt and glasses.

"Are you the father/son team doing the road trip that I saw on the news yesterday? It mentioned that you were planning to come visit us today."

"Yessir. I'm Greg, and this is my son, Andy." And stuck out his hand for a shake.

"Well, I'm Smokey and this is my place. I am thrilled to meet you. If you would follow me, I'll give you a behind-the-scenes tour and make sure you get fed properly."

They rolled through the kitchens and the smokers, and got to see what it was all about. They ended up in the dining room with all the brisket they could eat and were given T-shirts signed by all the staff.

After they were sufficiently stuffed and smoked, they said, "Thanks," and headed back to their hotel for a nap.

Later that night, they took an Uber to the show.

When they walked up to the "Will Call" window, the manager met them at the door.

In a drawl Texans are famous for, he asked, "Y'all are Greg and Andy?"

"Yessir."

"Welcome to the ACL. We are happy to have you here as our guests. We love what you are doing and have upgraded your passes. A little birdie told us you love tonight's performer."

"Yessir, that's right. He has always been one of my favorites."

"Fantastic. Come with me and I will show you to your seats. Y'all have front row seats now, as well as a backstage pass for the meet-and-greet before the show."

"What? Holy moly! Y'all are too kind. Andy, what did we do to deserve this?"

"I don't know, Dad, but I'm not gonna say no to it," he replied with a grin.

They enjoyed a wonderful evening that was truly memorable.

The next morning, they set out for the longest leg of their trip—the final one to Road America. They were figuring on a two-to-three-day drive, depending on how they were feeling, with a stop in Memphis, as it was on the way. There was so much blues and music history for Greg to enjoy.

They toured Elvis's house, and a night out on Beale Street, watching all of the local blues bands.

"I'm feeling pretty good this morning. I feel like driving," said Greg. However, after just an hour, his head was hurting, so they had to switch drivers. Greg took some of his meds and fell asleep in the back seat. It was later that afternoon when Andy pulled into the campground of Road America.

While at the gate, the ticket agent recognized who they were and asked, "Would you mind pulling off to the side there, for a moment? Someone would like to come greet you and get you all set up."

They pulled over and waited, then saw a golf cart rolling up with the crew chief of Clippity Clop Racing and the Director of Operations for the facility. Apparently, the chief had chatted them up to the director and asked him to do something special for them.

"Welcome to Road America. It's a pleasure to meet both of you. We have heard a lot about you and have been watching your vlogs. This is a wonderful thing you are doing together. We decided that we just had to do something fantastic for you. The chief tells me that you have never been in a racecar before. Is that right?"

Greg nodded his head.

"Yessir, that's correct. I always wanted to, just never knew anyone that had one."

"Does that go for you, too, Andy?"

"Yessir!"

"We are gonna fix that for you today. We have a couple of hot laps set up for each of you in a Cup car. How does that sound?"

Father and son were stunned. They looked at each other like this wasn't happening.

With big grins on their faces, they said, "Let's do it!"

The group headed down to the track and got suited up in fire suits and helmets. A few minutes later, they were screaming down the front straight at 130 miles per hour and headed for a fast left turn. Greg could not smile any wider. He was even ignoring the pain in his head right now. The adrenaline was blocking out the tumor's presence, he was having so much fun.

On Sunday morning, when the adrenaline and excitement had worn off, Greg's head was hurting more than normal. He was also dizzy and couldn't keep any of his breakfast down. A quick call to Dr. Collins was made, and Greg was ordered to take the next flight home. The director said they could leave their rig at the track and come back for it later.

Dr. Collins and Sophie were waiting at the airport when they landed and sped them to the hospital. After a few tests, they confirmed that the tumor had grown significantly, and Greg didn't have much time left.

The doctor left the three of them alone in the room to say their goodbyes. It was quiet for a while. From the hospital bed, Greg finally spoke up.

"Andy, these last four months have been the most fun of my entire life. I can't thank you enough for hanging out with me. It makes me happy that I got to know you as my son and as a man. I gotta go in a minute, and your mom and I have already talked. You will be just fine without that mean, ole boss you have."

With that said, he sat up and grabbed Andy's hand with all the strength he had left and shook it. Then he laid back down, closed his eyes, and went to sleep. A few minutes later, he flat-lined, according to the machines that were hooked up to him.

A nurse came in silently, turned off the machines, and left as quietly as she came in. Sophie and Andy sobbed as they held each other. They were comforted by the fact that Greg had gone out on his own terms.

A few weeks later, after Andy had returned from Road Atlanta with the truck and camper, he and his mom went to breakfast at their usual place. She handed Andy a letter.

Before they left on what was to be their best road trip ever, Greg had written a letter to him. It said that what money was left in the 401(k) that they didn't blow was all Andy's, to do whatever with as he saw fit.

Andy had the perfect idea of how to honor his dad, start a new career, and help other people all at the same time. With the funds, he created a nonprofit charity that offered trips to children and their parents who were in the same situation as the one his family once found themselves in.

About the Author

David Lastinger was born in Texas and currently lives in Phoenix, Arizona, with his wife, two dogs, and a cat. He has lived there long enough now to be considered a native. When he's not working or writing, you can find him on an outdoor adventure—typically cycling, hiking, camping, or kayaking. One of David's proudest accomplishments is that he and his best friend have completed the first 500 miles of the Pacific Crest Trail.

David has worked at various jobs throughout the years. He spent 20 years in the hotel business, 10 years as a self-employed auto detailer, 10 years in the mortgage business, and some time as a courier for a medical supply company. David has been writing as a hobby since his college days. Many of his stories come from those experiences and his chronicles of them. Some days, he's even glad he saved those journals.

This book of short stories is his second one but is the first in his short story series. His first book is titled *How to Do Things Your Phone Won't*, which is a self-help guide for anyone that is just getting out on their own and is currently available on Amazon.